The Chronicles of Henry Roach-Dairier:
To Build a Tunnel
by Deborah K. Frontiera

ISBN: 0-9753410-1-4

Library of Congress Control Number: 2004093107

Key words: 1. fiction 2. fantasy 3. insects 4. future worlds 5. young adult 6.adult

The Chronicles of Henry Roach-Dairier:
To Build a Tunnel
Second Edition

Published by Jade Enterprises
11807 S. Fairhollow Ln., Suite 106
Houston, Tx. 77043-1033
713-690-7626

Printed in the United States of America

Dedication: To Linda and Diane, my first fans, and to Dorothy, my agent, all of whom believed in me from the start.

Acknowledgements: Thank you to the many people in the Houston Writers League, the Houston Chapter of The Society of Children's Book Writers and Illustrators, my sister Besty, Carl, Charlie, and Harry, whose honest critiques helped make my writing stronger. Also, thanks to my husband, Jasper, for doing all the technical things for which I have no talent.

Special thanks to thesse professionals:

Cover art by Korey Scott, Denton, TX
Cover Design by Ira VanScoyoc, Emerald Phoenix Media, Manvel, TX

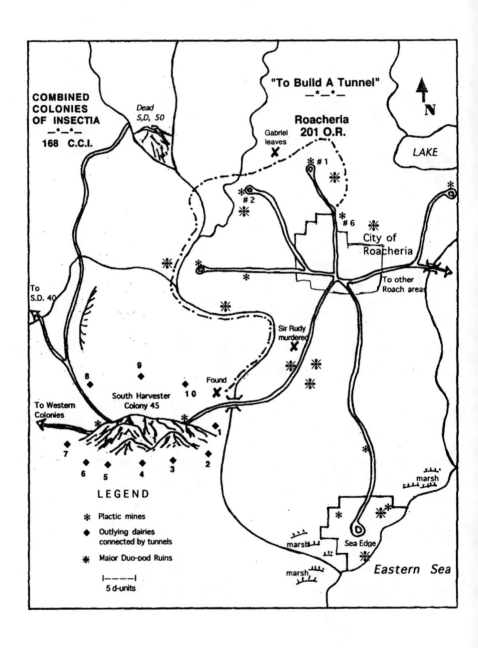

"To Build A Tunnel"
—*—*—

COMBINED
COLONIES
OF INSECTIA
—*—*—
168 C.C.I.

Dead
S.D. 50

Gabriel
leaves

Roacheria
201 O.R.

LAKE

1

2

6

City of
Roacheria

To other
Roach areas

To
S.D. 40

Sir Rudy
murdered

To Western
Colonies

9

8

South Harvester
Colony 45

10

Found

1

7

6   5   4   3   2

marsh

marsh

Sea Edge

marsh

Eastern Sea

LEGEND

✳ Plactic mines

◆ Outlying dairies
   connected by tunnels

✳ Major Duo-pod Ruins

|————|
5 d-units

N

Introduction

The Beginning:
as revealed to Daeira Dairier in dreams and meditation

In the beginning, Essence roamed the skies looking for the right place to start a world. She saw that our planet already had cycles of day and night, water and air. It had a set path around its sun so its cycles could be numbered, but it had no life.

"I will see what can live and grow here," she said, and joined herself with it. The Creative Life Force of Essence endowed the waters with miniscule plants and creatures and the cycle of life began.

Essence cherished this new life, but was tired from her journey across the cosmos, so she entered the earth and went to sleep.

Eons later, when she awoke, the planet was filled with life forms. The water and land and air teemed with a great variety of plants and creatures. Some were tiny and frail, others huge and fierce. There was great variety even in their coverings--smooth, hard, scaly, furry. The large, scaly ones dominated at that time.

Essence watched her world. The sun fed the plants, which fed the moving creatures, who then were eaten by larger ones, and on and on. They grew, propagated, and returned to feed the earth when their time was over. Some creatures failed and disappeared, but new ones evolved to take their place.

And ants were there.

Essence, satisfied with the balance and cycles, cradled her world, and went to sleep again.

The pain of many shocks woke Essence. Chunks of matter hurled through the cosmos and struck the planet, killing millions of life forms and knocking the planet in its cosmic path. The dust from their impact screened the sun's light, denying life-giving energy to plants. Essence watched in dismay as thousands of species disappeared from her cherished world. In her grief, she shook. Hills tumbled. Mountains sent forth liquid fire from within.

But even in grief, Essence's Creative Life Force found its way again. An infinite variety of flowering plants came to be. A few species of the scaly creatures and the small ones with fur and feathers survived.

And ants were still there.

Essence watched for many eons as the fur creatures increased in size and began to dominate. "What would happen," Essence said, "if I interfered and gave one life form an advantage? If I gave a tad of my intelligence to a creature, could it create something original, as I have?"

Essence looked closely at each species and finally chose one that seemed different from others. This species was not entirely covered with fur, stood on only two appendages, and had a well developed nervous system. She infused them with more intelligence and waited to see what would happen.

Season cycles passed. Generations of Duo Pods came and went. Essence saw that they made tools, built things, and developed the planet. Their machines grew ever more complex. Satisfied, Essence took a nap.

Essence awoke with a fever. The planet's surface was a shambles. The air and the water were fouled. All the Duo Pods, all of the feathered creatures, and most of the furry ones were dead forever.

"What has happened to my world?" Essence cried.

Grief for her failed experiment and illness consumed Essence. The earth shook. Storms raged. Her tears covered many lands. Then slowly, the earth healed itself. Although it would take many more eons for all of the Duo Pod creations to return to the earth, the world looked new and fresh once more. Essence found that one substance the Duo Pods had made would not break itself down and feed the earth. They had indeed created something original. Her experiment had not been a total failure.

She looked around hopefully and found that ants, roaches and other insects were not only still there, but had to grown greatly in size and changed in other ways.

"Ah, my faithful ants," she said. "You have been with me from the earliest days and have always been civilized. Perhaps the intelligence I gave the Duo Pods was not enough. I will try again. I will give you not only the gift of knowledge, but my compassion as well. And this time, I will not sleep, but will watch over my world. I will be available to my creatures, speaking to their minds when they seek me. When each one's time on earth is done, the part of me that is in them will return to me in unity forever. Eat then, my ants, of the lasting creation of the Duo Pods-- plastic--and receive my gifts. Cherish my world and seek to understand its mysteries."

And so we are.

While Essence was speaking, a group of roaches approached. They took the gift of intelligence, but ran away before the second, more important gift of compassion and inner essence was given. Thus they received no more of Essence than had the extinct Duo Pods.

Bemused, Essence observed the roaches as they ran from her. "I must watch and see what comes of this development."

Forward:
Henry Roach-Dairier

*W*hen I wrote about my grandfather, I had all my information directly from the original source, Antony Dairier. Not long after it was circulated throughout The Combined Colonies of Insectia, I received a package from my great-uncle, Andrew, who was my grandmother's youngest brother.

A brief note came with the package. "Dear Henry, I never knew my sister well, since she was thirteen season cycles older than I, and had been living and working in New South Dairy 50 for several season cycles before I emerged as an adult. I feel much closer to her now through your account. You honored her and Master Antony in the highest way. So I feel it is fitting that you should have these. Perhaps one day you will find it right to personalize this segment of antstory as well."

The package contained the journals of Uncle Andrew's parents, Henry and Adeline. I was pleased to accept them, since I am named for both my great-grandfather and my grandmother. The journals contained Henry's and Adeline's accounts of the season cycle Henry and two other ants spent building tunnels in Roacherian plastic mines under conditions that can only be described as slavery.

At the start of every term at the training facility in the City Of Roacheria where I teach Ant language and culture, I make it a habit to trace my family background, and how I, as a roach, came to be part of both the ant and roach worlds, and why I work so hard to help understanding between us continue to grow, after over two hundred season cycles of distrust. I tell the young roaches how my father came to be adopted by Antony and Henrietta after the last violent conflict.

Another term began right after I received the journals from Uncle Andrew. It took me by surprise when a new trainee named Ruth remained after the others had left, and asked to speak to me privately. In spite of the fact that many more females in Roacheria now receive formal training, she was one of only three females in the group. A few of the males had made snide remarks about them, until I stated my rules regarding insults and personal questions, and told them to leave if they couldn't follow those rules.

"Trainer Henry," she began, "my family lives in a very old domicile. Recently, my younger brothers had a fight and knocked down part of a wall. We found this between the partitions. My father said I should take this training unit and try to find out to whom it should be given. From what you said, you are one of them."

I looked at the words on the outside. "To the descendants of Henry, Herbert, and Howard, three tunnel engineers from South Harvester 45, only after Sir Rex Roach is dead, or no longer in control of the South East Roach Control Board, that they may know the truth."

It was also an account of the incident with my great-grandfather, but as experienced by a roach mine tunnel digger, Gabriel. The coincidence of receiving the two versions within such a short time span unnerved me. As I read Gabriel's journal, I was shocked by the depth of deception used by the roaches in convincing the ants to work for them. I wondered if the affair would have ended as peacefully as it did, if South Harvester 45 had known the truth at the time.

Ants keep journals for their descendants to remember and learn. Roaches do so out of a sense of self-importance and hide them carefully, lest the contents be used to condemn them for illegal activities. Gabriel's journal was obviously not written for those reasons. I wondered if Rex Roach, the villain of it all, had kept a journal. I went to the Archives of the Condemned to see about it. Rex *had* kept a journal, found only after his condemnation, when officials were sent to confiscate all his possessions. Since I am a descendant of one of Rex's victims, I was given access to it. It was there, in Rex's journal, that I found the seeds of deceit, greed, betrayal, and treachery which still sometimes trouble the relations between The Combined Colonies of Insectia and Roacheria.

After other research into the times in which they lived and much meditation on all four accounts, I give you *To Build A Tunnel* as true to the way they lived it as possible. Perhaps by presenting all the viewpoints of this unfortunate time, I can further nurture the seeds of healing.

1.

*Y*oung Rex Roach hurried toward the entrance of the Number 1 Plastic Mine, owned by his father, Sir Rudy, an influential member of The South East Roach Control Board, the governing body of Organized Roacheria. Several mine workers frantically attempted to clear debris from the tunnel's entrance.

Roacherian plastic mining was a half scientific, half luck affair. Plastic would be found on the surface and scavenged. When it was gone, digging would begin. The hole would be enlarged and deepened until the pit resembled a huge, bowl-shaped scar in the planet's surface, sometimes 2000 f-units in diameter. The depth varied greatly from one location to another. Tunnels would be dug into the slopes as needed. This particular mine had begun on the side of a slope, so its pit was comparatively small and its tunnel system much more extensive.

A confused noise of wailing and questions came from several female roaches, wandering about, searching for their mates and sons, to see if they had gotten out before the tunnel caved in.

Rex approached the workers. "Where is Gabriel? Did he get out?"

"Yes, Sir, he's over there resting," replied the overseer.

Rex moved toward where the mine tunnel digger reclined on the ground, front pods on his head, moaning. Parts of his back were caked with mud but Rex could see no obvious injury, which relieved him. Gabriel was not a great tunnel digger, but he was the best available in the area.

"What in maggot muck happened, Gabriel?"

Gabriel looked up and shook his front pods in anger. "Exactly what I told you would happen without enough support timbers! The whole thing fell in. Twenty, maybe thirty workers are dead because you wouldn't authorize more timbers!"

"Pah, on workers. I can get fifty more tomorrow and they'll be glad of the chance. How long will it take to get back on schedule with production? Every day is less credit."

"Do lives mean so little to you, Rex? Where will you get your workers when the shortage means nymphs will suffer from Plastic Deprivation? You won't have your luxurious life when they reach adulthood so mentally impaired that they can't dig in your mine."

Rex glared at him, eyes afire. He rose to his fullest height so that his six f-unit body--for he was one of the larger variety of roaches-- towered over the smaller, more slender Gabriel. It struck him as ironic that the plastic which made him rich was left behind by soft-bodied Duo Pods who, many thousands of season cycles ago, had stepped on and crushed ancient roaches. Now, he and his kind, evolved in size and intelligence, dominated and did the stepping.

He suppressed the urge to punish Gabriel. "I realize you are upset by your own narrow escape, so I will overlook your rudeness to me for the moment. Get up and come with me. My father wishes a full report immediately."

Gabriel rose, winced slightly, and reached back to rub the support joint of his back-left leg. He followed Rex up the path to the structures which housed the mine's administrative work chambers.

Sir Rudy stopped pacing as Rex and Gabriel entered. "How bad is it, Gabriel?"

Gabriel humbled himself before his powerful employer, stooping and sweeping his front pods outward in a submissive greeting. "At least sixty f-units collapsed. Between twenty and thirty workers are dead. If I'm given twice as many timbers, I can probably repair that section in two time frames, but the rest of the tunnel is just as bad. Unless I rebuild the whole thing, we're sure to have an even worse cave-in."

Sir Rudy groaned and crawled onto the softly padded bench behind his slanted work surface, dangled his middle and back legs in a resting position and tapped his front pod on the polished wooden writing surface.

"Why does it seem so impossible for you, or any roach tunnel digger for that matter, to build a tunnel that won't fall in without half a forest to support it? Do you think timbers are free? Five season cycles ago, I was inside South Dairy Colony 50, negotiating a plastic trade deal with those ants. There wasn't a timber in the place."

"With all due respect, Sir, if you want an ant tunnel, hire an ant, and get some of that miraculous tunnel liquid of theirs while you're at it." Gabriel's voice rang with sarcasm, but he didn't care.

Sir Rudy stared at him and softened his voice. "All right, Gabriel. You do the best you can with what we have. Go home. Get yourself cleaned up and tell that mate of yours you're all right. Take a few days off and have a physician check that obviously hurting back appendage. Send the bill here. We'll discuss this further when we're all in a better mood."

"Thank you, Sir," Gabriel said. He turned and limped toward the portal.

Sir Rudy turned to his first-hatched son after Gabriel closed the portal. "Learn one thing thoroughly, Rex. Look far ahead when you plan. Next time frame is not as important as next season cycle, or five season cycles from now. Learn to weather temporary set backs and bide your time patiently. I listened to Gabriel, ignored his disrespectful remark, offered to pay a medical bill, and sent him off happier. Now he thinks I'm great, and he'll settle for half the timbers he really wanted. Sometimes loyalty costs a little, but it's worth it later."

Rex tapped his back pod on the floor and sat silently, his abdomen protruding from the open back of the chair as he leaned against its wooden side.

Sir Rudy looked at him curiously. "What's in that scheming mind of yours?"

"I was thinking that he's right. We should hire some ants."

Sir Rudy broke into gales of laughter. "What maggot crawled inside your head and ate your brain?"

"No, Father, I'm serious. Hear me out."

"I'm listening," replied Sir Rudy, stifling his laughter at his son's serious tone.

"Remember when The Board was trying to negotiate with South Dairy 50 two season cycles ago for some tunnel liquid?"

"Yes, we offered three season cycles' plastic supply for the formula and the training to use it. Then before the deal was complete, **poof,** no more South Dairy 50. We lost our negotiators and a good interpreter."

"Why not try again with South Harvester 45?"

"South Dairy 50 needed us. That surface has no more plastic. I never understood what those ants lived on. Why do you think we head the banished in that direction? We know they'll be dead in a time frame. South Harvester 45 has its own mine."

"We just need the right incentive."

Sir Rudy shifted and twitched his antennae. "Such as?"

"Some phenomenal amount of credit."

"It wouldn't work. Ants don't work for their own gain. They work for 'the good of the colony,' or some such nonsense."

Rex persisted. "Every creature has a price. You taught me that. Who cares if they share it with their whole colony? We might imply, not promise, but imply, that plastic prices would drop if we had better tunnels. The whole southern region of The Combined Colonies purchases a little more plastic from us each season cycle. I think their population is growing and their production isn't keeping up."

Rex rose from his chair and looked directly into his father's face. "Once you and I get that formula, we could charge the other mine owners whatever we wanted and increase our financial empire a hundred times."

Sir Rudy stared at his son. "Well, I'll be... I haven't raised a fool after all."

"Take it to The Board, Father. It'll look more official on S.E.R.C.B. parchment, though The Board will know it's a private deal."

Sir Rudy nodded. "I'll make inquiries about a good interpreter this afternoon. Now, a chore for you. Get an exact list of the dead workers. Go to each family and try to be pleasant, even if you have to clench your mandibles. Give our condolences along with the rest of this time frame's pay and our standard death benefit. It's a meager amount, but they'll thank you. If they have any reasonably intelligent adults in the place, offer them the job."

Rex rose to leave. He detested going to the worker's domiciles. He never went to that part of the city unless he wanted a female without the responsibility of a mating contract and the bother of raising nymphs. His father didn't know half of what was in his cold, calculating mind, or just how devious he could be.

2.

*I*n one of the deepest sections of South Harvester Colony 45, Henry Harvester smoothed the last section of his training tunnel and scooped the rest of the rock and soil into the metal carrying basket. He brushed the dirt from his maroon shaded exoskeleton with his front pods and straightened his five f-unit body. Long ago, ants had been either red or black, but now so many were a mix of varieties (harvester, carpenter, dairier, or whatever) it was hard to say what any ant was, except for the fire ant guards. They were called one or another for their colony's origin, not for their genetics. Henry was proud of his blended shade.

He smiled with satisfaction and remembered the words his mentor, Master Andrea, had said when she assigned this final project. "You are to build a tunnel completely on your own. It must be at least six f-units wide, seven high, have one slope down on at least a twenty degree angle, one left and one right curve. There's plenty of room in the lowest part of the colony's south quadrant. You'll find other tunnel engineering trainees there doing the same thing.

"Tunneling is a science, but it's also an art that must never be lost. Use the science you've learned to create an artistic tunnel. You may ask me questions as you need to, but I will not see it until you tell me it's finished. Only then will your mentorship end and you be admitted to the colony's crew of tunnel engineers."

For six thorax-straining time frames of sixthdays and evenings, and an occasional seventhday, he'd labored, his leg muscles often aching with strain, as he hauled baskets fifty to seventy-five times his own body weight from the depths of the colony to the top of the mound. Because of it, when he saw pain in the eyes of the diggers and carriers working under him during the regular work day, he stopped them and told them to rest.

When he saw the first tell-tale hints of dust coming from a curved ceiling, he knew to shout an alarm before collapse occurred during construction. His ability to calculate the angles and curves, work quickly with numbers, forces, weights, and charts had improved one-hundred percent.

He smiled to himself again, now that he fully understood why he had been given this assignment, crawled beneath the basket, lifted the final load and hauled it to daylight at the top of the mound. An h-unit later, he led Master Andrea into his completed tunnel.

Most training tunnels were simple, dead-end affairs: in, up, down, left, right, end. Not Henry's. His had two entrances. It curved sharply downward in a tight spiral to a tiny chamber at the bottom. Then a wider spiral in the opposite direction brought one out again.

"You have the art, Henry," said Master Andrea as they stood together in the tiny chamber. "Will your family join me tonight at my domicile to celebrate the completion of your mentorship?"

Henry hesitated. "I have plans with Adeline this evening. I know tomorrow is Last Day, but would it be possible for you to join my family then? Adeline and her family will be there, too."

Master Andrea smiled. "Do I sense we will celebrate more than the completion of your mentorship?"

Henry laughed. He'd spoken of the depths of his feelings for Adeline more times than his mentor probably wanted to hear. Master Andrea read him like a manuscript. "Yes," he said simply. "I thought I would bring Adeline here tonight."

"A fitting place, since she has waited so long for you to finish it. My mate and I will be happy to join you tomorrow."

*   *   *   *

Adeline Harvester stroked her sister Deanna's larva. The small, white wiggler curled up against her thorax, soaking up the tenderness of her stroking pods, and dozed off. Even though she spent her work days in Northwest Larva Nursery 3, she still enjoyed caring for her sister's young one. Deanna had mated a dairier the previous season cycle, and shortly after this first egg had hatched, he had been killed as he and his partner defended their grasshopper herd from a mantis. Deanna needed the help and emotional support of her family, and Adeline had been living with her since then.

The domicile latch clicked and she heard her sister's voice. Adeline laid the sleeping larva in the soft thistledown of the larva coop, an oval shaped basket of woven reeds. Deanna entered the small sleep chamber. It's plain brown, gently curving, earthen walls seemed to cradle them as they talked about Deanna's visit with friends. A tapping at the portal interrupted them.

"I'll see who it is," offered Deanna.

Adeline gazed at the larva again, wishing it were her own.

"Hello, stranger," Deanna teased. "Adeline, Henry's here."

Adeline scurried into the parlor. "Henry, I didn't expect you so early. You haven't been here this early for..."

He finished her sentence. "Almost half a season cycle."

Deanna waved them both out the portal. "Go on, you two. Spend some time together. Don't wake me up when you come in. I'll get you up in time for Last Day meditation."

Adeline gave her sister an appreciative smile and closed the portal behind her. Henry took her front pods in his. "I have a surprise for you."

"You finished it?" she asked, following him down the tunnel.

"Yes."

Adeline knew her waiting was over. Three and a half season cycles ago, when they had both completed job exploration and begun their mentorships, Adeline had asked Henry to make a mating promise. She often recalled that day.

"Adeline," he had said, "you know I cherish you, but I wouldn't be fair to you if I made a promise now. My mentorship with Master Andrea will take most of my time. I wouldn't have many h-units to spend with you. You should be free to spend time with others. When my mentorship is complete, if you've found no one else you cherish, I will make a promise with you."

A season cycle later, when she had completed her own mentorship, she'd said, "Henry, there is no one for me but you. I've begun my life's work. We don't have to wait until you finish your mentorship."

And he had said, "I know many pairs mate while one is still in a mentorship, but I don't feel right about it. When I give myself to you, I want it to be totally. I want to be able to share in raising our young. I can't do that now. I'm lucky to have a little time to spend with you on seventhdays."

During the time Henry had built his tunnel, he had often fallen asleep as they sat together on the floor cushions in Deanna's parlor, while Adeline massaged his aching joints. Now he walked with a spring in his step and joy in his eyes. Laughing, they scurried down level after level, cheerfully greeting those they passed, until they stood before his training tunnel.

"Go ahead in," he said, pointing to the entrance of the slightly longer, outer spiral. "I'll be right behind you."

As soon as she entered, he ran down the tighter, inside spiral. When she reached the tiny chamber at the bottom, he was already there. Before she could speak, he took her front pods in his. "This is for you, for us. This tunnel is my promise to you. The spirals are our mating dance, and now I can give myself to you; for every bit of earth I dug and hauled out, I did thinking of you."

"You are worth waiting for. This is the most beautiful place I've ever seen."

Together, they rose to as full a height as they could, nearly standing on their back appendages, joined their middle ones for balance, and lifted their front pods above their heads (where they just touched the ceiling) and spoke the words of the mating promise.

Henry stroked her head and antennae, and swept his middle pods over her smooth, purplish-black thorax and abdomen. Since her abdomen was larger than his to accommodate eggs, he could not quite reach the end. "First day, when the new season cycle begins, I'll be working with a team on a new residential tunnel in the lower western quadrant. They've already begun some domicile work there. The first one on the left will be ours, and it will be complete in one time frame. That's how long it will take for the grassfrond seed ale my father and I will make to ferment for our celebration."

"You've got it all planned, don't you?"

"You waited for me. How could I do any less?" he replied.

<u>3.</u>

*S*ir Rudy handed his son a mug of ale.   "Here's to your appointment to The Board, and to our little 'ant venture!'   What a team we'll be in the future. Some Board Members laughed at your idea, but said good luck. They don't think the ants will go for it. The Colonies are still angry over the last time we demanded more food products for our plastic. But they also said we can use South East Roach Control Board parchment and conduct business as we please. What did you find out about that interpreter named Rufus?"

Rex took the ale and crawled onto a cushioned bench opposite his father. "Plenty. He's the best. He grew up near, but not in, the shanties. He's mostly self-trained and extremely intelligent. He used to work in plastic transport. His last trip was to South Carpenter Colony 12 three season cycles ago. When they met the ants for the exchange, the roller on the container slipped. Rufus was in the way and got crushed. The other transport workers thought he was dead and left him for the flies. Those crazy ants saw he wasn't dead, bound up his fractures and carried him back to their colony. Some surgeon glued him back together. Since we only make one plastic trip there each season cycle, he ended up living with them until the traders returned."

Sir Rudy filled his mug again and shifted his abdomen in the open back of his chair. "Where are his loyalties? With us or the ants?"

"I'm getting to that. He learned the language and their ways. When he got back a season cycle later, he realized he could earn more interpreting than he ever would in transport. He got himself a better domicile and took on a mate. Now he has a pile of debts because he bought a better life on credit he hadn't earned yet. He's eager for more permanent work than he gets in document translation and communications. Best of all, he knows all the right things to say to ants. In other plastic deals, he's managed to cheat the ants out of huge amounts and come out smelling like blossoms. He's loyal to those who pay him."

"How much does he want?"

"He said he would only negotiate that with you. He should be here any minute. I sent for Gabriel, too."

"Have Gabriel wait outside until we have an understanding with Rufus. Send our female attendant for more ale and refreshments," Sir Rudy said, rising from the chair and sauntering about the chamber.

Rex rose from the bench, opened the portal and called out, "Get off your lazy abdomen and bring some ale and a platter of fried flies eggs and sliced grasshopper. Send Rufus in as soon as he gets here, but have Gabriel wait until we ask for him."

He turned back to his father. "That skinny little female makes my head swim."

"Well, forget it. You know I don't like your patronizing the lower employees. Stay out of the shanties. Find yourself some well-bred female and mate properly, Rex."

"Mates are a bother. They're always trying to tell you what to do."

"Your mother never did."

"That's because you kept her in her place. Now, most females think they should have half of what a male owns. Some fool told them how ants hold their females above everything and it got all blown out of proportion. Your so called 'well-bred females' think we ought to worship their abdomens and pamper their every desire. I want a female who serves me, not the reverse. Even Regina and Rolinda are starting to get arrogant."

"Your sisters are only nymphs and are still grieving for their mother. Enough of this subject. Keep an eye on Rufus. Signal me if you think he will do right for us."

Sir Rudy returned to his chair. The attendant entered, carrying a tray of food and a jug of ale. She set the food down on the surface in front of Sir Rudy and refilled his and Rex's mugs. "Should I pour a third, Sir?"

"No, that will be all."

She stooped low and left the chamber. In a moment, she returned with Rufus and closed the portal, leaving the three males alone.

Rufus bowed low and swept his front pods out to the sides. "Interpreter Rufus, here at your request, Sir Rudy."

Sir Rudy tipped one antenna in acknowledgment and pointed to the bench next to Rex with his front pod. He flicked one back pod slightly outward, a signal to Rex that he should keep quiet, listen and learn. Rufus seated himself on the cushioned bench next to Rex and eyed the food.

"Rufus, you come highly recommended. I appreciate your meeting with me on a seventhday," Sir Rudy began. "Let me tell you a little of what I have in mind, and then you tell me how you would do it. I want to negotiate an agreement with South Harvester Colony 45 to hire two or three tunnel engineers to rebuild the tunnel into my Number 1 Mine, and train my tunneler in the use of that stuff they call tunnel liquid. I'd like to offer them a large amount of credit for plastic, but only pay a small amount, if any. Let them think it's for about six time frames, but actually, I want to make it permanent, so I can rent them out to other mine owners. I want to start immediately. Can you leave at dawn tomorrow with a letter to negotiate? I'd like to be in that colony talking to them through you on secondday."

Rufus tapped his back pod in thought and swept his front pod to the top of one antenna. "It can be done, Sir. The amount offered should read something like, 'up to whatever amount of credit for plastic, less living expenses.' In an ant colony they don't pay directly for things. They take what they need at their markets and records of use are kept. In the rare event that someone should take too much, that ant is asked politely to remember his fair share and the good of the colony. They have no idea what things cost here. You could charge anything you like for living expenses and they wouldn't know until it was too late."

Sir Rudy chuckled gleefully and pointed toward the platter of food. Rufus nodded his head in thanks, filled a container and continued. "Second, you offer to pay upon completion of satisfactory work. Ants are fanatics about pleasing others. You keep finding fault with their work, and they keep fixing it to fulfill their obligation."

He stopped a moment to eat a slice of grasshopper. "Make sure you request unmated males. Ties to a mate are very strong. You can justify not wanting females by saying that we lack proper facilities for larva care. They're very different from nymphs and need their plastic finely ground and mixed with honey dew, a very complicated formula."

Sir Rudy looked at his son. Rex's expression remained the same, but he made a small circle on the floor with his back pod.

"More fly's eggs, Rufus?"

"Yes, thank you, Sir." He paused a moment to chew. "Don't send me tomorrow, because it's Last Day."

"What's Last Day got to do with it?"

"Last Day is a very solemn occasion for ants. Only medical workers and those on the dairies who handle grasshoppers and aphids work that day. They trade off, so they have half a day to complete their rituals. Their council will not receive me on Last Day."

Sir Rudy set down his mug of ale. "Then you better not plan to have much ale Last Night. If it isn't good for you to interfere with their solemn occasion, then leave early First Day and give up your own holiday." He looked at Rex again, who made another small circle with his pod.

"You're asking a lot, Sir Rudy. What are you offering?" Rufus eyed the decorative objects in the chamber.

"If you negotiate this deal and we leave South Harvester 45 with my engineers, and their council is happy, I'll pay you half of what you earn now in a season cycle. In addition, I want you to continue to work for me, translating between the ants and my tunneler every day. For that, I offer twice what ever you're getting now."

Rufus nearly dropped the fly's egg he was eating.

Rex straightened up in surprise. Although he still lived at home, sharing his family's luxurious life and not having to provide for himself, he put in many long h-units at his father's command. His personal fund was not that much. He swallowed his irritation over the amount and said nothing. He could play his father's game, and his own plans would soon show who was better at it.

"Sir Rudy, I am at your service," Rufus said.

"Good. I want you to express urgency when you meet with them. Tell them I'd like to arrive there at noon on secondday, complete the negotiations as soon as possible, and be back here with my engineers by fifthday at the latest. I don't want them to have time to think about it."

Rufus rose, stretched out his middle and back legs, then let them dangle over the sides of the bench. "That won't be a problem. I'll tell them about the grief of the families who lost males in your recent collapse. I'll say that nymphs will suffer for lack of plastic as long as the mine is closed, and that this is our most productive mine. They don't know exactly how many mines we have in the southeast region, and providing all young with plastic, regardless of family status, which they don't have as we do, is a high priority for them. When you're there, whatever you say, even if it's an insult that they won't understand, use a subdued tone of voice, as if you really care about those families. Think of your lost profits and act like you're grieving. I'll appeal to their sympathy and charity."

"Charity?"

"It's their belief that they should all take care of each other, Sir."

"How convenient. It makes deceit easy doesn't it?"

Rufus nodded.

"One more thing, Rufus. Everything said here today is in strict confidence. You will be my highest paid employee, and I don't want that getting out, or the actual details of my plans. If anything does become public, I'll know who to blame, and you won't like the consequences."

"I understand you perfectly, Sir Rudy."

"Then let us seal our agreement without parchment."

He poured a mug of ale and offered it to Rufus. Rufus bowed his antennae, drank some, and set it down again. Sir Rudy motioned to Rex, who picked up the mug, drank, and offered it to his father, who finished it off.

Sir Rudy went to the portal himself and told Gabriel they were ready for him.

"How's that back appendage, Gabriel?" Sir Rudy asked him.

"Getting better, Sir. My joint is strained, but not broken."

"I'm glad to hear that, since you will make a journey with me soon. Seat yourself and have something to eat."

Gabriel crawled onto the last cushioned bench and reached forward timidly for the few remaining morsels. Sir Rudy rarely offered him anything, especially not expensive delicacies like fly's eggs or imported grasshopper. He wondered what this unexpected hospitality meant.

"Gabriel, you should speak in anger more often. Sometimes, such statements turn out to be good ideas. My son and I plan to take your advice and see about hiring some ants."

"Sir, forgive me... I didn't mean that you should..."

"Don't look so worried. I don't intend to replace you. This is Rufus, by the way," he said, gesturing toward the interpreter. "He speaks Ant very well, and the day after tomorrow he'll carry an offer to South Harvester 45. I hope to have some expert ant tunnel engineers work here for an extended time. If the ants' first response is positive, I want you to go with me on secondday to complete the arrangements."

Gabriel looked at Rufus. Although the interpreter's slender brown body was marred by numerous scars, he radiated confidence. Unsure of himself, Gabriel said softly, "Why do you want me to go?"

"I want you to see what I've been talking about, tunnels with no support timbers. Look carefully. I want them to teach you what to do."

Holding a slice of grasshopper, Gabriel asked, "How would I do that, Sir? I don't speak the language."

"Rufus will work with you. Watch what they do. Make drawings, charts, whatever it takes. Later, I'll expect you to be able to teach others."

"I don't know what to say."

"Say you'll do it. I'm making a sizeable investment in your training, Gabriel. You'll be very valuable to me when it's over and I'll expect your gratitude."

"Of... of course," Gabriel said, lowering his head and antennae.

"I will, naturally, increase your earnings when I see results. There is one problem I would like to avoid. If these ants come, which I'm sure they will; and you learn well, as I trust you will, given your level of intelligence; you might consider yourself valuable to other mine owners. I would hate to lose my investment. You will sign this document stating that you will not leave my employment for any reason. I will decide which mine owners will receive your services and control your work completely."

"But what if you decide my work is unsatisfactory?"

"If I decide to end your employment, any agreement we had would be void. You would be free to work for anyone who wanted you."

"Sir Rudy, I am honored that you consider me worthy of this opportunity," Gabriel said, thinking of the job security he would have and the possible prestige involved.

Sir Rudy handed him the document he had already prepared. Gabriel, Rex, and Sir Rudy signed and dated it. "Seventhday, 28th day of the 13th time frame, 200th season cycle of Organized Roacheria."

4.

*E*arly Last Day morning, ants gathered in large groups in the various communal meditation chambers throughout South Harvester Colony 45. Henry left his domicile and hurried along the tunnels until he came to Deanna's portal. Both females were ready and Henry offered to carry Deanna's larva.

When they arrived at Meditation Chamber #5, Henry whispered to Adeline, "Next time we have Last Day, it will be our larva I'll carry."

Adeline smiled and reached around to stroke the back of his thorax with one middle pod. The three of them joined the other members of Adeline's family, resting their abdomens on the padded bench, middle and back legs on the floor in front of them. They raised their heads and thoraxes to look toward the lightning bug lamps at the front of the chamber and joined front pods with those around them. Vibrating mandibles hummed a melancholy tune then sang:

Lament At The End Of The Season Cycle:

Chances gone by and not taken
Words of kindness not said

The many forgotten things
Time gone by, time gone by
May never be regained

Chances taken and lamented
Words we said that caused pain
Wrong choices made in haste
Time gone by, time gone by
May never be undone

Then they chanted their creed: "On this Last Day, as we link one solar season cycle to the next and unite it with the thirteen lunar time frames, we remember that all things are linked to each other.

"Creator Of The Universe, and all its cycles, and infinite variety of living things, we offer up our thoughts and dedicate ourselves once again to all that we believe.

"To us has been given the gift of knowledge and the wisdom to discern right from wrong. May we reach out to help each other carry the responsibility of this gift.

"We pledge to respect all living things and the delicate balance of the chain of life; to take care of the planet and seek full understanding of its many cycles; to take no more than we need; to replenish what we take and reuse what we have; to cherish our mates and families and care for each member of every colony, placing the needs and good of others above our own.

"Help us to meditate upon how well we have lived this creed; to seek pardon of anyone we may have offended; to generously forgive all who may have offended us; and to resolve to live the new season cycle even more fully. So be it."

The shades on the lightning bug lamps, which had glowed very low until that point, were opened a little, symbolic of the increase in daylight as each new season cycle began. The ants remained silent, each one lost in his or her own uplifted thoughts for nearly half an h-unit before the shades were fully opened, bathing the chamber and its occupants in light.

"As the daylight increases, so does our resolve to live our lives in simplicity and charity."

Those in front picked up baskets of grassfrond seeds and passed them around, one for each two ants. The unusually large seeds, about a third of an f-unit each, were broken and shared.

"May the All Powerful Force, which makes the grassfronds grow from a large seed to a great height in a single season cycle, nourish us now with this seed. May we grow with it to care for each other more fully," they recited before eating the seeds.

The meditation service ended as it began--in song. But the mood of the song was different:

Praise For A New Season Cycle:

Learn from the pain of yesterday
The future will be what we make it
Choose this day to grow in care
Sing praise for all that we can share
New creatures we all can be

Erase all the pain of yesterday
Nothing can change the past
Rejoice in the chance to change
Sing praise for tomorrow yet to come
New creatures we all can be

They left the assembly and headed for their homes, exchanging cheerful greetings.

Henry's parents hosted a large group in their humble home. They placed extra, borrowed floor cushions all around the edges of the parlor to accommodate their grown young and their mates and larvae, Adeline's parents and her sister, and Master Andrea and her mate.

"It's good to be around larvae, now that my youngest is pupating," said Master Andrea.

In the center of the parlor lay an oval cloth of finely woven thistledown. It was covered with baskets of toasted seeds, platters of succulent roasted grasshopper, shredded plastic salad, jugs of honey dew, fried fungus and fungus muffins, and freshly baked ant bread. Everyone had brought something. Joy swirled through the chamber as they embraced one another, stroking each other's antennae affectionately before beginning the feast.

Master Andrea rose as they finished eating. "It is with great happiness that I return this to you, Henry. Congratulations." She handed him his training contract, a document in which he'd pledged himself to her for a period of three to four season cycles, "or until all requirements of the tunnel engineering program are completed."

Across it she had written, "Most favorably completed," and the previous day's date, "seventhday, 28th day of the 13th time frame, 167th season cycle of The Combined Colonies of Insectia."

Henry bowed his head in humility and accepted it. The others showed their pride by rising in silent respect around him. As he raised his head to speak, they reclined on the floor cushions.

"Thank you, Master Andrea. You have been my mentor, my friend, my confidant, and my encourager. You listened to my problems, my hopes and my dreams. You were a patient guide, and I hope that, one day, I will pass on the same knowledge to others. Now I would like to announce that I have given myself away again, this time to Adeline with a mating promise. We hope all of you will share the joy of our ceremony on sixthday, the twenty-seventh of the First Time Frame."

Pods drummed the floor in approval. Henry's father began to laugh, "I thought you two made your promise long ago."

Adeline explained. "I guess you could say we had a promise to make a promise."

Henry's mother picked up the slicer and began cutting a large honey cake. She passed the pieces all around. "It's truly satisfying to end the season cycle with such joy."

5.

*E*vening shadows turned to darkness when Rufus returned to Sir Rudy on Firstday, breathless, but smiling. Rex did not have to be reminded to offer him refreshments.

"I see you have good news for us," Sir Rudy said. "Sit down and rest yourself."

"They will see you tomorrow, Sir," Rufus puffed between gulps of ale. "I arrived a little before noon. I spent nearly an h-unit with several members of South Harvester 45's Council, explaining your request and going into a lot of detail--which I made up-- about the collapse. They reacted as I hoped they would, sympathy for the families and all that. They gave me food and drink while I waited for their chief tunnel engineer, some female named Master Andrea, to come. She asked me a lot of questions I couldn't answer, a lot of technical stuff. She was rather skeptical. I kept apologizing for my lack of knowledge and told her that Gabriel would be with us when I returned, and I was sure he could satisfy her concerns. I didn't leave until way past mid-afternoon. I scurried at top speed all the way back."

"Well done, Rufus. You'd better head home and get some rest. You live near the old west sentry post, don't you?"

"Yes, Sir."

"No sense traveling across the city to come here, only to go back again. I'll meet you at the sentry post at dawn."

Rufus left. Rex closed the portal and turned to his father. "You should take some of our personal warriors with you in case of bandits."

"Not this time."

"Should I send some on fifthday to escort you back? What if some other mine owner, like Sir Rollo, resents your accomplishment and tries to abduct our ants as you return? You know how jealous he's always been of you because of our mine's productivity."

"First, they don't think I can negotiate this deal. Second, they won't be prepared for my return so quickly. I left the impression that I wouldn't leave until next quarter time frame. I specifically mentioned next thirdday. But I think I'll leave the main trail before we reach the west sentry post, travel through the meadows outside of the city, and come straight here to the mine. You should look for us by an h-unit after noon at the latest. I appreciate your concern. Security will be needed once it's known we have them."

Sir Rudy crossed the chamber and drew back the heavy, woven window covering. He looked across the mine pit to its opposite side. "That old Duo Pod ruin is fairly stable, isn't it?"

"Yes, the synthetic stone is still strong."

"Doesn't it have some underground chambers?"

"Yes, Father, I believe it does."

"Tomorrow, gather a crew and clean up one of the underground areas. That ought to make our ants feel at home. Supply it with some cushions, work surfaces, parchment, and ink, good lightning bug lamps, and all that. Don't make it luxurious, but at least as decent as Gabriel's work chamber. Since they'll live there as well, get some sort of portable sanitation facility. Get a good, strong, portal installed with some sort of locking mechanism. Double the guard at the mine and assign ten warriors to that edifice. If they are well guarded, our competitors can't get them, and they can't go slipping away from us either."

"Perhaps I should assign fifteen, not ten."

"Whatever you think. I'll be sure to ask the ants to bring any tools and implements they use that we don't have. I wonder what sort of storage facility they'll need for that tunnel liquid, and how difficult it'll be to transport."

"Maybe the ants will carry it themselves. They can lift a lot more than we can," Rex reminded him.

"I know, but if it's too bulky, I think I'll get it shipped later. Let's head for home. The next few days will be long and busy for both of us."

*   *   *   *

Secondday, Sir Rudy rose very early and breakfasted on fly's eggs and seeds. He owned several ornaments on chains that signified his rank and importance as a member of the South East Roach Control Board, which he hung over his head. They dangled below his mandibles in a way that would catch any creature's eye immediately.

Rex handed him a satchel. "I packed all the S.E.R.C.B. parchment and ink you'll need, Father. Do you want me to go to the west sentry post with you?"

"No. I want you to see to the preparations for our ants. Don't talk to anyone about my absence."

"Good luck, Father," Rex said, tipping his antennae respectfully.

Rex watched his father disappear into the darkness, down the pathway that led from their elaborate domicile, and into a larger pathway through the city. Then he headed in the opposite direction, slipping between the wood plants and tall, decorative grasses that grew around the stately living areas of important roaches in that part of the city. On he went, through less attractive areas and finally to the eastern edge of the city near the shanties where a huge wood plant grew.

The tall conifer stood alone at the edge of the sprawling area of ramshackle homes of Roacheria's poorest, a refuge for criminals and renegade warriors who sought work as mercenaries. He looked carefully around, twisting his antennae in all directions. When he was certain that no one was about, he tacked a small piece of parchment to the tree.

"Small band of warriors needed for one time operation. Group commander should be on the north side of Bush Row one h-unit past midnight, thirdday."

He drew back and concealed himself behind some bushes. Several scrawny roaches looked at the parchment and then passed on. Rex knew they would find someone to read it if they couldn't. As the cloudy winter sky turned from black to gray, a surly old warrior approached the wood plant. Rex looked at him carefully, noting his markings. The warrior glanced around, took the parchment and scurried off.

*   *   *   *

Sir Rudy saw Rufus and Gabriel waiting for him as he approached the west sentry post. Both stooped low in greeting. Sir Rudy nodded in return. Board appointed warriors sometimes stood guard there to watch for bandits or renegades, but things had been quiet for a time, so no one was in the sentry post. The three set off on their journey.

The path meandered across a huge area once inhabited by Duo Pods. Piles of rubble dotted the meadow grass, small wood plants and bushes often growing from them. Here and there, larger, more sturdy edifices of synthetic stone reinforced with steel stood out like gaunt sentries. Some towered high above the meadow grass.

The city of Roacheria sprawled amidst the north and east sections of the ruins. Other Roacherian communities dotted the fields and coastal plains all the way to the sea and along its shore, in and around other areas of ruins, wherever plastic could be found.

Gabriel attempted conversation. "What fascinating creatures they must have been."

"Who?" asked Sir Rudy.

"The Duo Pods. They must have been remarkable to build such things as these. I find the artifacts in the public viewing area of our science facility quite interesting."

"If they were so great, why did they die off? Once they trampled ancient roaches. Now we walk on their remains. I have but one interest in this place--plastic. This area was scavenged off ages ago. It's worthless now. I support the archaeologists financially for one reason. Some day they may find something that tells us how plastic was made, or a better way to find it underground. When they do find it, I'll own it, since I pay for their projects. Because of me and others like me, The Board won't let the ants into this area either. We don't want them finding something first."

His bluntness let Gabriel know he did not wish a contrary opinion. Gabriel let his mind wander. The scenery was unchanging, d-unit after d-unit of meadow grass, brown and dry in this season, small wood plants and bushes, some bare, others holding their leaves throughout the season cycle. Occasionally, a small, furry creature darted into a hole in the ground, and they did see a few giant crickets, but over all it was bleak. Maybe Sir Rudy was right. It was just worthless surface area.

The distance from the west sentry post to South Harvester 45 was between twenty-five and thirty d-units, two and a half to three h-units travel at a moderate roach pace. However, Gabriel's back appendage was still bothering him, so the three of them made frequent stops to rest.

Sir Rudy paced impatiently during the fourth stop. "We'll never get there at this rate."

"I'm sorry, Sir," Gabriel said. "I'll try to go faster. I didn't realize how much it still hurt until we had traveled a bit."

Rufus offered an alternative. "Let me twist several grass stems together and bind it up. You can travel on five pods."

Gabriel found it awkward, but less painful as they continued. Toward the west edge of the ruins, they crossed a wooden bridge over the steep-banked stream marking the boundary between Organized Roacheria and The Combined Colonies of Insectia. Since times were relatively peaceful, there were no roach warriors or fire ant guards on their respective sides.

They saw an outmound shortly after that. Rufus called out in Ant, "Greetings, it is I, Rufus, who passed this way yesterday. I have returned, as I said I would, with two others."

Several fire ants rose from the grass both in front and behind them. Gabriel wondered how long they'd been watching. Rufus talked to them. They brought out a large carrying basket.

Rufus turned to Gabriel. "They noticed your discomfort. Get in the basket. They will carry you from here."

Gabriel climbed in. The ants reached out their pods in support and spoke softly. The tone in their voices reassured him, even though he did not understand the words. He wondered at such kindness to a total stranger, and a roach besides.

When they entered the huge mound of South Harvester 45, Gabriel looked around in awe. The main tunnel sloped gradually downward. A steady stream of ants came up, carrying baskets full of soil and rock. Other ants carried baskets with a variety of products in and out. The tunnel was very wide and quite high. He hadn't really believed what Sir Rudy had said, but here he was, and he couldn't see a support timber anywhere.

The ants led them down several levels through slightly smaller tunnels until they came to a large portal. Rufus spoke to several ants who greeted them with smiles and cheerful sounding voices. They entered a comfortable chamber. Two ants served them roasted grasshopper, toasted seeds, and honeydew.

"Whatever else I may think of ants," Sir Rudy whispered, "no creature can prepare grasshopper like they can."

Rufus introduced Sir Rudy and Gabriel. Gabriel gawked in surprise, for the female who had served his food so humbly was Alyssa, their Council Chief.

Rufus turned to Sir Rudy. "We will begin the discussion shortly, when Master Andrea, the tunnel engineer I told you about, arrives. Remember to use a somber tone of voice, no matter what you say."

To Gabriel he said, "You don't have to act; you already look pitiful."

Master Andrea arrived with a stack of parchment. She looked at Rufus and asked, "Is this your engineer?"

Rufus nodded and introduced them. Master Andrea seated herself opposite Gabriel, smiled and said, "I'm pleased to meet you. I'm anxious to know what methods you use to build your tunnels."

Rufus translated.

Gabriel said, "I'm afraid our methods are very bad. I direct the digging and shore it up with timbers as we need them." He took some of the parchment and drew a sketch.

When Rufus had translated his comments, Master Andrea stared at his sketch, hung her head and groaned. "No wonder your tunnels fall in. Don't you use any calculations?"

When Rufus translated this statement, Gabriel gave her a blank look.

She took out parchment, wrote down an equation, handed it to Gabriel, and said something to Rufus.

"Gabriel, she wants to know if you have had any training in computation. This is sort of a test. She wants to see if you will even be able to learn their methods. If you can't do the calculations, there is no point in going on."

Gabriel looked at the writing. Ants and roaches used the same number systems, and he had done problems like this in advanced training. He had no trouble working it out. When he handed it to her, she nodded and handed him more. They handed the parchments back and forth. Rufus gave up translating for the moment. The problems were far beyond his ability, and they seemed to be communicating well with drawings and numbers. Master Andrea's expression changed from the skeptical, business-like one she'd had when she entered, to a pleasant smile.

She drew one of the parabolic graphs over the sketch Gabriel had done of the square tunnel shored up with timbers. "You know how to calculate these things. Why don't you use this in tunneling?"

When Rufus had translated, Gabriel replied, "There is so very much I want to learn from you. That's why I came. Will you be able to teach me these things in six time frames?"

"It will not be me. I have others in mind." She turned to the ant council members, spoke with them, and then waited while Rufus translated.

"Sir Rudy, she says that Gabriel can be taught their techniques and will probably learn them quickly. She has three engineers in mind, two to do the tunneling, and one to teach Gabriel each step. She has not spoken to them yet. We will meet them tomorrow."

"Ask her about the tunnel liquid," Sir Rudy said.

"Sir, I didn't bring it up yesterday."

"Bring it up now."

Rufus addressed Alyssa and Master Andrea. The ants' mood changed. Gabriel wondered what was going on. Sir Rudy tried to interrupt, but Rufus gave him a signal to wait. Gabriel used the time to look carefully at the chamber around him. He noted the smoothness of the walls, the gentleness of the curves, the height of the chamber in relation to its depth and width, and began to make a sketch.

Finally, Rufus turned to Sir Rudy. "Sir, they will not even consider giving us tunnel liquid. They say that the kind of soil in plastic mines does not require it. They only use tunnel liquid for going through rock layers, or for hardening the walls of very large tunnels, such as the one we first entered. It's not used for most smaller tunnels. The second reason has to do with safety. Tunnel liquid is apparently very caustic and dangerous. Plastic mines sometimes contain toxins and other dangerous substances. They worry that tunnel liquid may hit some poisonous substance by accident and react unexpectedly. The death of South Dairy Colony 50 two season cycles ago reminded them how easily tragedy can happen when creatures are not careful with things of the ancient past. They do not wish us to have any disasters."

"You can't convince them otherwise?"

"No, Sir, that's what I've been trying to do. She wants to take us on a tour of the colony, and show us tunnels that have been built without the liquid."

Sir Rudy looked irritated.

"Sir," Gabriel said, "I think we should listen to them. If I can learn their techniques, our purpose is accomplished, isn't it?"

Sir Rudy lifted his pods in frustration. "Tell them we will take the tour."

The ants offered to carry Gabriel. He accepted humbly, for his sprained appendage was still throbbing with pain from the journey. He didn't pay attention to the conversation as they proceeded down several levels. Instead, he looked carefully around him at the details of the curves, trying to burn everything he saw into his memory.

He also noticed that every ant he saw had a job. At one place he saw two cleaning a tunnel and picking up containers of refuse. It wasn't the sight that he found unusual (Roacheria had its refuse collectors) but the way they were treated by those with him. In Roacheria, such workers would hurry to get out of the way of a more important group. Sometimes, they would be roughly pushed aside. The ants, however, waved greetings. The tone of their voices was cheerful. Alyssa even stopped and helped them a moment before the group went on.

When they reached the deepest part of the colony, Master Andrea explained that this was the place where engineers in training worked at tunnels on their own and didn't use any tunnel liquid. Through Rufus, she told the roaches how this was done. She invited them into several, pointing out the smoothness of the tunnel walls and their strength. Sir Rudy was impressed, but Gabriel was amazed.

As they got ready to leave, Sir Rudy pointed to one more entrance. "What about this one?" he asked, going right in. Before the others could react, he disappeared completely, then reappeared a few moments later in another place a few f-units further down. "Who is the genius who built this? I want him. Why did you skip this one?"

After Rufus translated his statement, Master Andrea replied, "Rufus told us yesterday that you wanted only unmated males. We understood your reasons and agreed with them. The builder of this tunnel is promised to someone and will celebrate his mating very soon, so I didn't think you would consider him. That's why I did not show you that tunnel."

Rufus explained in Roach to Sir Rudy. "This one is promised in mating. You don't want any with other commitments."

"What do you mean by promised? Is he mated or not?"

"Well, Sir, technically, he's not mated, but for them, a promise is as good as mated. The emotional bond is already there. Believe me, Sir, you don't want the complications this will cause in your long term plan. Take my advice and forget this one."

"If he's not physically mated yet, I want him."

"Wait. Let me explain. You know how it is when you have a daughter, and you have arranged a mating contract with a suitable male. You protect that daughter, until all the legal papers have been signed, so that the male will take responsibility for any nymphs. Then you get them together physically as soon as possible. Their promise is a little like that period of time, but longer. Some ants wait a season cycle or more between the promise and their formal mating. They're different from us. Our females are fertilized once for life and all young belong to the first male who takes her, but a male can be with many. Ant males can only fertilize one, so they are pretty careful about giving themselves. Believe me, Sir, there will be a bond between them that will complicate your plans."

He turned back to Master Andrea and said in Ant, "I am not trying to be rude. I was explaining your mating customs to Sir Rudy."

Sir Rudy was quiet a moment and then said, "He can wait and stay promised for a while. I still want him."

"Master Andrea, Sir Rudy would very much like to meet the builder of this tunnel. He would like to ask him if he would consider coming to teach us, even though he is promised. Is it possible for him to consider waiting a while to join his mate?"

Master Andrea sighed. "I will speak with him this evening, but you must realize that he may choose not to go with you, or his Promised One may not give her permission. Come, I would like to show you the tunnels in our plastic mine."

By the time the tour ended, both Gabriel and Sir Rudy were convinced that the science of tunneling was more important than tunnel liquid for their purpose.

"We will take you to our guest quarters now," Alyssa said. "You'll find supper prepared for you. Two council assistants will arrive tomorrow at eight h-units to escort you back to the council chambers. The engineers will join us at that time and we'll finalize our agreement."

"That's very gracious of you," replied Rufus. He turned to Sir Rudy and whispered, "Have you ever stayed overnight in an ant colony?"

"No."

"Please, don't complain about the accommodations. To you, they may seem inappropriate for someone of your rank, but you must understand that their leaders take no more than the lowliest colony member. What they will give us is about the same as Alyssa has. Don't lose this deal for yourself by changing your tone of voice now."

So Sir Rudy kept still as they entered their quarters. Gabriel found nothing to complain about. The parlor was fairly spacious. Images of the colony mound covered with blossoms in the spring decorated one wall. Floor cushions, lightning bug lamps, and flat surfaces for working or eating filled the open area. At one end of the main chamber were two small sleep chambers. Each had two thistledown mattresses with brightly printed coverlets. A sanitation facility joined the two sleep chambers. An area for food preparation lay at the other end of the parlor. Ant bread, warm honeydew, and a serving dish filled with a mixture of seeds, cooked roots and chopped grasshopper lay on the eating surface.

The ants left them in peace.

"You two sleep together. I'll take the other chamber," Sir Rudy said. "I can't believe they all live like this."

Rufus and Gabriel didn't argue. Sir Rudy ate quickly, complemented the food, and seated himself at a writing surface to prepare his final proposal.

Shortly after, a young male ant arrived and explained to Rufus that he had come to treat Gabriel's sprained appendage.

"Why are they making such a fuss over me?" Gabriel asked.

"I... sort of made you a hero yesterday," Rufus explained. "I told them you saved three workers, and that was how you were injured. I said that in spite of it, you still wanted to come with us. Accept the treatment. They're very good, and it's free. I know what I'm talking about."

"Rufus," Sir Rudy called out, "write this in Ant in your best script and make several copies. Hide the things you need to as we discussed."

The ant laid warm packs on Gabriel's joint, massaged it gently, and gave him a mixture of herbs in warm honey dew to drink. Gabriel thought about how he had been injured. He had run to save his own exoskeleton, tripped and gotten trampled by others. He hadn't saved anyone. Instead, one of the workers had picked him up. Though he grieved for the families of the dead, Gabriel knew he was a coward, not a hero.

The treatment felt wonderful. The ant left a packet of herbs and told Rufus how to mix it with warm water for Gabriel to drink in the morning. Gabriel decided that there was more he wanted to learn from ants than the science of tunneling.

6.

*H*enry and Adeline sat in Deanna's parlor, curled up, sipping warm honeydew. Deanna called from her sleep chamber, where she was putting her larva down for the night. "All right, you two, not so close. Now that you're formally promised, I have to act like a chaperone."

The teasing tone in her voice started them laughing.

"Someone is tapping at the portal," Henry said. "I'll get it."

He rose and opened it. "Master Andrea, what a surprise. What brings you here? Come in."

"Your parents said I would find you here. How is it going with the residential tunnel crew?" She asked, greeting both of them fondly.

"Fine, but it's only been two days."

"Henry, I don't quite know how to begin, and I'm glad I'm able to talk to both of you, since this involves a possible delay in the date of your ceremony." She paused and sighed. "You are aware that we are hosting some roaches for a few days, and that they want some of us to teach them how to build better mine tunnels."

"My team leader mentioned it today. What does that have to do with me?" He motioned for her to recline on one of the floor cushions.

"At first, it had nothing to do with you. They said they wanted unmated males." She explained some of the discussion that had already taken place; the decision not to send tunnel liquid, and the tour for the roaches. "This Sir Rudy, who is a bit pompous and obviously accustomed to getting what he wants, invited himself into your tunnel. It was evident that he admires talent, which you have plenty of. He wants to meet you and ask you to be one of the three going with them for six time frames."

"But I can't. Our ceremony... I wouldn't dream of putting it off."

"I know. I told him through their interpreter that it wasn't my decision. If I didn't consider this terribly important, I wouldn't even be here." She told him all of what Rufus had said the day before: the collapse, the description of grieving families, and Gabriel's heroism. "The interpreter, Rufus, spent a season cycle in an ant colony. He has learned our ways and seems very sincere. I'm even more impressed with their engineer, Gabriel. I tested him thoroughly this afternoon. He knows the math and he's very intelligent. He just doesn't know how to use the calculations to build a tunnel. I don't know why they don't teach them that way. This is a good opportunity for trust to begin between the roaches and us. They are finally saying that we may know something they don't. The council agrees that we should make this arrangement."

Henry curled one middle pod around Adeline's thorax. "Who else is going?"

"Your friend, Herbert, and Howard, whom you've never met. He's been working mine tunnels for many season cycles. His mate died last season cycle and his only daughter has been mated and on her own for a long time. He's offered to go as a last job before he retires. I chose Herbert and he agreed. He isn't seeing any particular female right now, and he's almost as talented as you are. He's been on Howard's team since he finished his mentorship."

"Then why me?"

"To teach Gabriel. They say the interpreter will work with all of you. You sketch well and so does Gabriel. You won't need to translate the math. I found Rufus bothered me more than he helped as I tested Gabriel today."

Henry straightened up and lifted his front pods. "How am I supposed to teach him in six time frames what it took me three and a half season cycles to learn?"

"You only have to teach him to build one kind of tunnel, not every type of tunnel under every imaginable set of conditions. I cannot demand that you do this, but I wish you would think about it. It would be good for the colony and I know you can do it well."

She turned to Adeline. "I hate to ask you to postpone your ceremony after all the time you've already waited for Henry, but please, talk about this together. You don't need to decide tonight. We'll meet at eight h-units tomorrow in the council chambers. I hope you'll come, if only to listen to what they have to say. The final decision is yours, Adeline."

"We'll talk about it, Master Andrea," Adeline replied.

"Thank you. I'll alert your team, Henry. If I don't see you there tomorrow, I'll understand."

"Who will go as the third if I don't?" Henry asked.

"I had Dennis in mind until Sir Rudy saw your tunnel." She embraced them both again and left.

Henry wrapped himself around his Promised One. "I don't want to leave you, Adeline. We've waited so long already. I want to be with you now."

"I know. Personally, I don't want it either, but think of it from another point of view. What if that collapse had occurred in our mine, and families here were grieving? What if it were our young who might suffer from Plastic Deprivation? Think about that roach she mentioned, Gabriel, risking his own life to save three others. Isn't he worthy of being taught safe methods for building tunnels? Perhaps we need to think more of others and less of ourselves. Didn't we renew our pledge to do that on Last Day?"

"Are you willing to wait another six time frames, then?"

"I don't know, but I think we should go tomorrow and listen to them."

*   *   *   *

Rufus sat between Gabriel and Sir Rudy the following morning. As he watched the ants enter the conference chamber, he noted the young female and whispered to Sir Rudy, "Trust me, Sir, it would have been better not to request the one who is promised. He's brought her with him. Watch your tone of voice. She is the one we must convince, but I still advise you not to take that one."

"Stop worrying. I can play your game. She'll find another when he's been gone a few time frames."

"Don't count on it."

Gabriel looked at all of them, wondered who would teach him and awaited formal introductions. As soon as everyone had reclined comfortably on the padded benches around the conference surface, Rufus began. He introduced Sir Rudy, Gabriel, and himself to the ant engineers.

Master Andrea introduced the ants. She spoke slowly and paused often so that Rufus could translate. "This is Howard, one of our most experienced engineers. He has been building mine tunnels for over thirty season cycles. On my left is Herbert, who finished his mentorship two time frames ago. He has been working with Howard's team since then. Both are willing to undertake this project. Last, this is Henry, whose tunnel so fascinated you. With him is Adeline, his Promised One. I'm sure they have many questions they would like to ask you before making their decision."

"Most of your questions will be answered in the document you see before you," Rufus said. "Perhaps you should all take time to look over Sir Rudy's proposal."

Henry had not met any roaches, but he had heard many things. Sir Rudy, seated confidently opposite him, fit the pattern he'd been told about. Gabriel was different. Henry could see a genuine longing in his eyes that made him wonder. He felt Adeline curl one of her middle appendages around his and turned his eyes to the document in front of him.

"Great grassfronds," Henry whispered to Adeline. "Did you see the amount of plastic he's offering? That's enough to see a hundred larvae clear through to adulthood!"

"Yes, I wonder why they're offering so much. That's far too much credit for three to work for six time frames."

Henry barely saw the rest. His mind was filled with how much he would be able to help the colony with an amount like that. He turned toward Master Andrea. "Why didn't you tell me last night how much they were offering?"

"I didn't know. This is the first time any of us has seen the actual offer. It certainly is generous, but I have some concerns." She turned to Rufus. "What does this mean, 'less living expenses?'"

Rufus was prepared. "That is the amount the three engineers will need to live in Roacheria. Our system is different than yours. Of course, we would not expect them to go to the markets by themselves. Our market workers would not understand their requests. As a service, all their needs will be delivered to them, for a small fee of course. Each time frame, they will be given a statement showing their living costs to that date."

"What kind of lodging will be provided?"

Rufus turned to Sir Rudy and related Master Andrea's question to him.

"Tell her my son is preparing comfortable living quarters very close to the mine, in the hope that they will be occupied. Tell her that we felt the closeness would make it easier for them, and that we plan to accompany them daily to the mine to work, so they never need to worry about anything."

Adeline twitched her antennae after Rufus had translated Sir Rudy's statement.

Sir Rudy turned and said to Rufus, "Compliment the young female in some appropriate way."

"Adeline, or is it Master Adeline?" Rufus said smoothly. "Sir Rudy wishes to thank you for coming today, and for considering the possibility of allowing your extremely talented Promised One to undertake this project. He extends his congratulations to you."

She smiled. "It's just 'Adeline', and he is welcome. I would like to ask how often letters will be delivered. Would it be possible for Henry to come back for a short time half way through the project, or might I visit him?"

Rufus turned to Sir Rudy. "She wants to know about letters and visits."

Gabriel looked intently at Henry and Adeline as Rufus and Sir Rudy discussed Adeline's request. He could sense a strong bond between them. He thought of his own mate. She did not look at him with that kind of feeling and never had. He envied them. He also felt uneasy. Little things that passed between Rufus and Sir Rudy hinted that they were not being completely honest. But then, most roaches never were.

Sir Rudy said, "Tell her that she can write all the letters she wants. The traders can take them each time frame on their regular trips, but tell her that visits would be difficult. Make up something about how busy they will be. I don't know how you should say it, but make it clear there will be no visits. You know why."

Rufus hesitated. "The traders will be able to take any written communications on their regular trips. Personally, I would advise against your trying to visit. Those who work the trade routes are quite crude. They have no respect for females and would not treat you like you should be treated. I would not wish that experience on my own mate. A journey by yourself would be even more dangerous. The ruins are full of wild creatures and predators, as well as some of our banished criminals. I would hate for any misfortune to befall you."

He poured on the flattery. "I know it will be difficult for you to part, and that you will be making a tremendous sacrifice if you allow your Promised One to go, but you would only make your parting worse by doing it twice with a visit. I'm often apart from my mate because of the nature of my work as an interpreter, and she cries each time. Don't give yourself more sorrow than is needed. One parting, one reunion--the time will seem to pass faster that way."

"If the ruins are so dangerous, what protection will you have on your own journey back?" asked Alyssa.

Rufus was a fast thinker. "We will be met a few d-units inside our surface area by Sir Rudy's personal warriors. I was escorted by them coming and going two days ago. They are the best. They know every spider's lair and are well trained to chase off a mantis. Renegades and criminals run whenever they see his warriors."

Sir Rudy tapped Rufus. "What are you talking about now?"

"Don't worry about it, Sir, trust me." He turned back to the ants, "Are there any other concerns?"

"Not at the moment," replied Alyssa. "Would you mind if we took some time by ourselves to discuss this further? Perhaps you might take a stroll to the top of the mound until lunch."

"We would be delighted," said Rufus.

When the roaches had gone, Alyssa spoke first. "I don't see how we can refuse this proposition and remain true to our beliefs. Never before have I heard of such a large offer from a roach."

"That's exactly what bothers me," said Master Andrea. "It's too much. There is something about Rufus that troubles me, but I don't know what. I wish they weren't in such a hurry. I would prefer to send this proposal to the Intercolonial Council and ask their advice."

"That would take far too long," Howard said. "It would be a quarter time frame before the fastest carriers could get it there. Then more time would pass while they discussed it and sent a reply. We must make this decision here and now. For my part, I am ready to sign it."

Herbert said, "I'm willing to accept it for the good of this colony, and I will give all my funds to the colony treasury."

Henry couldn't focus his mind entirely on their discussion. He felt wretched inside, for he knew that he did not want to do what he should. Everything inside him screamed to tell them he refused to go, while a deeper part said quietly that he must. He and Herbert had been friends for a long time and he knew Herbert was right about putting the good of the colony ahead of his own desires.

He also knew Dennis. Dennis was a good engineer, but not very patient. Henry couldn't picture him explaining a tunnel curve to someone who couldn't speak his language. He looked at Adeline and could see in her eyes the same inner torment. She had been able to speak of duty and selflessness last night, but her pod shook as he held it.

Beneath the table, he stroked her back leg with his. "All my adult life I have been taught to put the needs of others before my own. If my colony now asks me to go, I will."

Alyssa looked at Adeline. "Are you willing to postpone your mating so Henry can be a part of this?"

Adeline did not trust her voice. She only nodded.

"Ours is not an easy creed to live. The Colony greatly appreciates your sacrifice and accepts your service, Henry."

When the roaches returned for lunch, Sir Rudy, Henry, Howard, Herbert, and Alyssa signed the agreement. Rufus politely asked Adeline for her consent. She nodded, but didn't sign the document. It was dated two ways, since each species numbered the season cycles from the time they'd begun their present forms of government: thirdday, First Time Frame, 168th season cycle of the Combined Colonies of Insectia; and thirdday, First Time Frame, 201st season cycle of Organized Roacheria.

The rest of the discussion centered on when they would leave, what things the ants would need to take with them, and what Sir Rudy would provide. Sir Rudy pressed them to leave the following morning, but gave in and agreed to fifthday. He declined any more colony tours, saying the three roaches would rest in their quarters, or wander about the nearby surface on their own.

7.

*R*ex waited until after dark thirdday night. He placed a container of light brown paint and an applicator in a plain satchel he'd already filled with plastic exchange notes, and then concealed the satchel under a cushion in his private chamber. A cricket-leg calling device hung by the portal. Its rasping noise as he rubbed the two parts together brought a domicile worker to him immediately.

"Yes, Rex, what is it you wish?"

"Tell Regina and Rolinda I'm very tired and will not join them this evening. See to it that their needs are provided," he said, stifling a yawn.

"Of course, Rex, anything else?"

"Make sure I am not disturbed before morning."

A few moments later, he looped the satchel around his front leg and slung it over his back. He crawled out the window of his chamber, climbed down the vines growing on the wall, and disappeared into the night. Half an h-unit after that, he arrived at his first destination, the back portal of one of the sturdier looking dwellings in the shanties. He looked around carefully and cocked his antennae. Sure that he had not been seen, he tapped on the portal. An attractive female about his age opened it.

"Rex, what a surprise. I haven't seen you in quite a while. What's wrong with my front portal?"

"My father has been going on again about my personal life and has had me followed lately," he lied. "I didn't want anyone to see me."

"Come in. What have you brought me and what pleasure is on your mind?"

Rex entered the domicile, which was much better on the inside than one might expect. She was well liked by many rich males, good at giving pleasure, and they provided her a living in return. Rex plopped himself on a cushion and took a wad of plastic exchange notes from his satchel. She took them from him.

"My, aren't we generous tonight. Planning to stay until dawn?"

"No," he replied. "I have a different request." He took out the paint and its applicator. "I'd like you to paint a light brown stripe down the back of my thorax with dash lines to its right."

"Whatever for?"

"That's not your concern."

"Anything else?"

"Perhaps, after the paint dries."

She picked up the applicator. "Down the middle?"

"Yes."

In a few minutes she had finished and handed him a looking glass. She held a second one behind him as he adjusted the angle of his to see her work.

"Good," he said.

She laughed. "You could be a twin to Sir Rollo if you were older. Do you want something to eat while it dries?"

"Yes. How would you know about Sir Rollo's markings?"

"Silly, he comes here at least once a quarter time frame," she said, handing him a bowl of crisp fried bee's wings. The two of them munched and talked for an h-unit, and Rex revised his plan slightly in his mind. It was fortunate that she had mentioned knowing Sir Rollo. He would miss her pleasure, but he could take no chance that she might mention this night to anyone.

She touched his back gently with her pod. "The paint is dry," she said, tipping her antennae and reclining on a nearby floor cushion.

With perfect calmness, he picked up a smaller cushion and moved toward her. In one swift movement, he pounced and pressed the cushion over her, blocking her air supply. There was a muffled cry and she struggled beneath him for several minutes before going limp.

He went to the food preparation area and quickly found a sharp cutting tool. He slashed the main support joint of her mid-right pod. Since she was already dead, not much life juice flowed out, but it would be enough. Then he slipped the tool into her left-front pod, which he knew was her dominant one.

When The Enforcers found her, they would pass it off as one more desperate female who couldn't bear to face another day. It was a common occurrence. The inquiry would go no further.

Rex picked up the paint container, the applicator and the plastic exchange notes. He looked carefully around to make sure he left no sign of himself and slipped out the back portal. Three lanes over, he stuffed the paint and applicator into the bottom of a community refuse bin.

His time piece told him it was an h-unit before midnight. Leaving the shanties behind, he lumbered off into the fields east of the city until he came to the place known as Bush Row where a long, straight line of thick bushes grew. It was a favorite meeting place for those who wished to hire renegades, because two could talk with the bushes between them to provide some anonymity.

A single Duo Pod ruin stood on the north side. Rex supposed there had been others once, as there were little piles of rubble all about the area. The one standing had been built of synthetic stone. He placed the satchel in the corner of an inner chamber and returned to the south side of the bushes to wait for the renegade who'd taken his note from the conifer.

At precisely one h-unit after midnight, he heard a sound on the other side of the bushes. He altered his voice to sound like Sir Rollo. "If it interests you, read the message you took from the conifer."

The warrior read his notice and asked, "What job do you have?"

"Fifthday, a certain conceited Board Member will travel through the western ruins toward the city. You'll know him by his ornaments. With him will be two other small, skinny roaches, and, hopefully, three ants."

"Ants?"

"If there are no ants, stay away and let them pass. I will contact you again some other time. If the ants are with the Board Member, attack and kill the Board Member, but don't, I repeat, don't, harm any of the others. Take them prisoner."

"Where do I deliver them?"

"Look behind you. Do you see that ruin? As a sign of my seriousness, go there now and you will find the first half of your payment. Don't run off with it, because I know who you are. Return here and I will give you more instructions."

Rex waited for the warrior to return.

"A very profitable offer," said the warrior. "What other instructions do you have for me?"

"Secure your prisoners in that same ruin fifthday, and you will find the other half. There is a row of bushes like this one ten d-units down the trail from the west sentry post. You and not more than ten should wait there to carry out this plan. Do you know the place?"

"Yes, it's very familiar."

"I don't know exactly what time this Board Member will pass, so have your band in place by dawn. Do not fail."

"Only an idiot could fail this job. One lazy, old Board Member, two small, nearly defenseless roaches and three stupid ants, well within our surface area, against ten of my best and strongest warriors is an easy take, Sir."

"Don't be too sure of yourself," warned Rex. "I know who you are. I'll see you sent to the mantis compound for your many crimes if you fail."

"Be assured, I won't fail. I didn't get my reputation from failing. Besides, those who hire me know that if I'm caught, I'll take my employer with me to my doom."

Rex was counting on that fact, and knew the renegade would watch as he left Bush Row. He was glad the sky was clear. The sliver of a moon and the stars would show off the painted markings. He lowered himself, back to the bushes, and crawled slowly into the night, mimicking the movements of one he knew well and despised.

As soon as he could, he rolled in a patch of mud, scurried home, climbed up the vines and crawled in his window. Quietly, he washed off the mud and the paint and cleaned up every last trace of his absence.

8.

*A*deline sat in Henry's sleep chamber at his parents' home, watching him pack. Both of them were quiet. There was so much, yet so little to say. Adeline looked around at the shelves, the charts on the walls, and the large slanted work surface where Henry spent so much time sketching tunnel designs. He managed to keep a lot of things for his work in this small space. She had often pictured an extra chamber in their own domicile, specifically for his work.

"Here," she said, handing him a couple of manuscripts from one shelf. "You'll need these, won't you?"

"Oh, yes," he said absently, taking the computation manuscripts from her and putting them into a second satchel. He had already filled one with parchment, his best drawing tools, a sliding bead calculator, tunnel charts, an image of Adeline, and other personal items. "I'm a little hungry. Would you like something?"

"Yes, I would."

They went through a short passage leading to the kitchen. "It was kind of the nursery supervisor to let you spend today with me," Henry said as he got out some roasted seeds and honeydew. It was the fifth time he'd said it since she'd arrived. He set down the container of honeydew and wrapped his appendages around her. She reached up and stroked his antennae.

"When you spoke yesterday about putting others' needs before our own," she said slowly. "I wanted to say it, too, and mean it, but today I don't know... I've thought so many times about how other colony members have given up their own desires... So many we read about when we started basic training... I never realized how much it hurts."

"We have today. It wouldn't be wrong. We could go and record ourselves in the Record Of The Mated. We could make my tunnel our home for a day, instead of waiting. Would that make you happy?"

"No, it wouldn't. I had that option on my mind all last night. That might seem like a good way to say good-bye, but it would only make us more miserable later. It would rob of us of the true joy that we should have. We would mate in sadness. Later we would regret that we had not had a ceremony and celebrated with our families and friends. Besides, you'd miss our first hatching. I see how my sister hurts, being alone. I don't want that. I would rather wait and truly be joyful."

"My father says the ale gets better the longer it ages."

She drank the last of her honeydew. "Oh, well, Deanna will be glad to have me around for a while longer."

"Let's get our minds off of it. As soon as I finish packing, let's go to the Leisure Center and play a few rounds of Ride-a-Hopper. We haven't done that in a long time."

Adeline smiled for the first time that morning. "Yes, that would be fun. I have one more thing for you to pack." Adeline went into the parlor for a moment and took something from the small satchel she had been carrying when she arrived. "My mother brought me this last evening, right after she heard you were going. She said she and my father were apart for a few time frames when they were promised, and told me that every night they each wrote in a journal about the day and what they would have said to one anther. They exchanged them when she returned from her journey. I have one just like it." She handed Henry a bound manuscript with blank pages.

"What a kind thought. Tell your mother I really appreciate it. Such beautiful binding," he commented, looking at the cover design, a pair of butterflies rising toward the sun.

South Harvester 45 had several Leisure Centers. Each one was a large open chamber. Padded benches and flat surfaces ringed the walls. Many different foods and beverages were available at five booths. Several game stations occupied the center. Some involved thinking out various strategies for surface survival, like tracing one's way out of the maze of a spider's lair. Others involved remembering facts in various areas of knowledge, or races in problem solving.

However, the most popular game in dairying or harvester colonies was the "Hopper Ride." A fair-sized, domed enclosure contained one or two nearly full-grown grasshoppers. The objective was to see how long one could stay on the grasshopper's back as it bounded about the enclosure. Sometimes, just getting on was a victory. Thistledown and dry leaves covered the floor for safety when someone fell. Those who worked on dairies were the best at it, but they never bragged to those who lacked such training. They were more likely to teach others what to do, so that the fun of it could be enjoyed by all. If a hopper seemed to be getting too tame, it was replaced with a new one.

The centers were quite crowded in the late afternoon and early evening, or on a sixthday, when young, unmated adults didn't have training or were through with their work day. Since Henry and Adeline arrived shortly after noon on a regular work day, there were very few others present. They headed for the hopper enclosure.

Henry rode the hopper first and managed to stay on for a few moments before he slipped off and landed in a tangle of leaves and fluff. Adeline stayed on longer by gripping tightly with all her pods. Henry did better the second time. They went back and forth until they were breathless, and then retired to a padded bench near one wall.

They were surprised when Rufus and Gabriel entered with a council assistant. Rufus saw them at once and came over to them. "We felt the need to relax, too," he said. "I had to show Gabriel that you creatures do know how to have fun."

"Try the Hopper Ride," Adeline suggested.

"No, I'm sorry, I can't," Rufus explained. "Most of the season cycle I spent in South Carpenter 12, I was recovering from my injuries. I was told to avoid things like this, even though the floor is cushioned, because I could refracture my exoskeleton easily. But I would enjoy watching you."

After watching them for a short time, Gabriel told them through Rufus that he thought it looked like great fun, but he had better not risk injuring his joint again.

Rufus moved away. "Come on over here, Gabriel. I think these two would rather spend the time by themselves."

Henry and Adeline walked over to a food vending booth. They asked for fried fungus and whipped honeydew.

"You know, they're different from what we've been told when you get to know them," remarked Adeline as she ate. "Master Andrea is right, this project may be a very good thing. I feel better now."

"I do, too," Henry replied.

*   *   *   *

Rex headed over to the edifice which would house the ants. The workers had finished and were ready for him to inspect the chamber at the end of a narrow, underground passageway. Upon entering, his first thought was that he was glad he would not have to live there. The synthetic stone was drab and lifeless. The cushions he had ordered provided the only color, not that he really cared. It felt cold, but then it was winter.

He examined the portal carefully. The wood was about four tenths of an f-unit thick. Its frame wedged tightly against the synthetic stone. A long, thick wooden pole fitted into two notches chipped into the stone walls of the passage, as effective a barrier as anything in the Detention Facility. Remembering that ants were very strong, Rex directed several of the workers to push against it as hard as they could from the inside.

Satisfied that his ants wouldn't be able to force it open, he made a mental note to himself to remind his guards to watch for any indication that they might chew through it. He had heard that carpenter ants could still gnaw through wood and hoped that none of those his father would bring had any carpenter antcestors. Would Rufus remember that? He had certainly know better than to allow any fire ants. If there was one thing roaches feared, it was the venom in a fire ant's sting.

Rex recalled what he had learned as a nymph. Early in the evolutionary process which had increased the size of all insects and brought intelligence to ants and roaches, ants had, for the most part, lost their aggressive nature. Fire ants were among the smallest of ant varieties, but they were still extremely fierce. Their mandibles could penetrate any exoskeleton and their sting was lethal. They never initiated conflict with Roacheria, but defended The Colonies mercilessly.

Since ancient roaches had lived around Duo Pod (and thus plastic rich) areas, they had kept control of them. Of the two varieties of roaches who had survived and developed on this land mass of the planet's northern hemisphere, the leaders who had formed Organized Roacheria had been of the larger variety, like himself. Their outer mandibles and their size had allowed them to dominate other roaches, and in the beginning, some ant colonies as well. However, after the ants formed The Combined Colonies of Insectia, the roaches lost that advantage, because there were fire ants in every colony.

The roaches began to use trickery to gain economic control. They took advantage of the ants' need for Roacherian plastic. Now, with Rufus to interpret, Rex could take advantage of their creed of selflessness. He would show The Board how to gain complete control again, and he would dominate The Board as well.

As Rex was leaving, his father's chief personal warrior, Ganton, approached. "Young Sir, I've arranged for the extra guards you requested here at the mine. There is a scrawny indigent over there who insists on seeing you."

Rex sighed. "I suppose he's looking for work."

"He wouldn't say. Shall I send him away?"

"No, I'll humor him. Where is he?"

"There," Ganton replied, pointing toward the rim of the mine.

"Come with me."

The two of them approached the roach.

"You have my attention for one minute. What do you want?"

The roach lowered himself nearly to the ground. "Forgive my appearance, Sir. Could we be alone?"

"This is as private as you'll get."

The roach looked fearfully at Ganton. "I'm nobody important, Sir, so I often hear things that are not meant to be heard. Sometimes that information is of value to others."

"Tell me what you came to say and I'll decide if it's of value or not."

"A certain renegade I know is bragging that he has another job to do. He was rounding up a small band. I heard him say to one of them that they were going to attack a Board Member and some ants. I was cleaning the Board Meeting Chamber when your father told The Board he wanted to bring ants here to your mine."

Rex remained perfectly calm. "Have you told anyone else what you heard?"

The roach remained in a submissive position. "No, Sir. That might get me killed. I risked myself coming here to you."

"Then you certainly will not go back and tell this renegade that you told me, will you?"

"Of course not, Sir. Then I couldn't gather information for you or others in the future."

"Get up. You're information is valuable."

Rex turned to Ganton. "Take our little informer to the clerk and get him my father's standard payment, then meet me in my father's work chamber."

He walked away from them and proceeded to his father's chamber. This unexpected spy made things even better. No matter which way this ended, he would have his father's worst enemy for conspiracy. By the time Ganton arrived, he had worked out the crucial timing problem.

"Ganton, I was afraid of this," he said as though genuinely worried. "I tried to tell my father he should have an escort on the way back. He would have no part of it; practically forbade me to send you."

"Your father has his own mind, Young Sir, but it is my sworn duty to protect him. I should meet him anyway, and prevent this thing. There's a chance this spy is saying it just to get your credit, but I won't take that chance."

Rex paced about the chamber. "Perhaps there is another way. What if you watched from a distance, kept my father in sight as he returns, without his knowing you were there?"

"An excellent idea," Ganton replied, raising both front pods.

"Do you know a good place from which you could watch? Perhaps some tall ruin along the trail?"

"Yes, about nine d-units from the west sentry post there is a tall ruin. You can see a long way from there."

Rex was delighted. It was the very spot he had in mind. It stood a little less than a d-unit from the row of bushes where the renegades would be hiding. Ganton would watch the whole thing and be powerless to stop it. He would reach the bushes in time to rescue Gabriel, Rufus and the ants.

"How many of our guards could you take with you?"

"As many as you want. It's got a large open space near the top and it's very stable."

"Take twenty, no, thirty. Go about midmorning," he instructed, "That'll be about two h-units before my father should pass there. Guard my father well! Do away with any who dare to threaten my father; and if there is a leader, see to it he is brought to justice."

Ganton bowed respectfully. "I am at your command, Young Sir."

9.

*F*ifthday morning, Henry, Howard, and Herbert met once more in the Council Chamber. Each carried two satchels. They greeted one another and seated themselves to wait for the roaches to arrive.

"Is Adeline coming to see you off?" asked Herbert.

"No," Henry replied, his voice shaking. "We said our farewell last night. I asked her not to come this morning. I might change my mind if she did."

Herbert placed his front pod reassuringly on the back of Henry's thorax. "I really admire you, Henry. If I had been in your position, I don't think I would have agreed to this."

Howard reached out a front pod as well. "I know it doesn't seem that way now, but believe me, the time will pass quickly. We'll be home before you know it."

Their conversation was interrupted by the arrival of the roaches. Sir Rudy entered with a confidant air, all his ornaments jingling against each other as they hung beneath his outer mandibles. Gabriel looked refreshed and cheerful. He declined the offer to be carried, saying his appendage didn't hurt at all now.

Rufus grinned. "Good morning. Shall we get started? Is this all you have to take with you?" he asked, pointing to the satchels that the three ants carried, as though he expected them to have more.

"This is all we should need," replied Howard. "It doesn't take that many manuscripts and tools to build mine tunnels, and you've said the rest would be provided for us."

"True enough," replied Rufus. Sir Rudy spoke to him. "Henry, Sir Rudy wants to know if we will see your charming Promised One again. Should we wait for her?"

"No," Henry said, more steadily this time.

Master Andrea and Alyssa joined them briefly to say farewell. They headed up the main tunnel toward the surface.

After they crossed the bridge and entered Roacherian surface area, Sir Rudy turned to Rufus. "Did you ask Henry if he'll miss the first hatching? I'll bet anything he mated her last night."

"No, I didn't. That would be considered an extremely rude and personal question. If I had asked him, he might have been offended enough to back out of the deal. I promised we'd leave the colony with them happy."

"I'm still curious."

"Please, stay that way. If he wants to say something, he will on his own. I would bet they didn't. Ants are very proper when it comes to their mating traditions."

"Ask him in some polite way," Sir Rudy said, reaching out to pluck a tuft of grass near the edge of the trail. "I'll bet you half a time frame's credit I'm right. I'll know by his expression if you tell me the truth."

"You're on," Rufus laughed.

Gabriel stared at them.

Rufus turned to Henry and said in Ant, "Gabriel and I really enjoyed watching you yesterday in the Leisure Center. Adeline is quite good at riding the hoppers."

"Yes, she is," replied Henry. "She's always been better than I at such things."

"Did you stay long after we left?"

"We stayed for a while. Then we had supper with her parents."

"A pleasant evening?"

By the look in Rufus' eye, Henry sensed what was really on his mind. He didn't like where the conversation was going. His voice was sharp. "No, Rufus, it wasn't. It was very difficult for both of us. You've told us you have a mate. Think how you feel each time you leave on a journey. I made an agreement with you and you wanted unmated males. I honored that agreement. When you learned our language, didn't anyone tell you it is very rude to ask such a personal question? I don't feel like discussing last night."

Rufus practically fell over himself apologizing. "Henry, please pardon my ignorance. I was not implying anything. I was only trying to make pleasant conversation. Please, forgive me. I probably don't fully understand what is considered personal and what isn't."

Henry calmed down. "It's all right. I guess you meant well."

An awkward silence followed. Then the roaches began their own conversation.

"Henry, try not to be so sensitive," said Howard. "A roach is a roach, after all. They'll never really understand us."

"They could try. We certainly try to understand them," Henry replied.

Herbert changed the subject. "Howard, have you ever traveled the surface much? I find myself wondering about a lot of things. My only trips to daylight involved dumping a load of dirt at the top of the mound."

"Long ago, before I began my mentorship in tunnel engineering, I spent two time frames with the carriers on the route between our colony and South Dairy 50, but that hardly qualifies me as an expert."

"Tell us what you do know."

Howard began to name some of the plants they passed, and told them about a time they had encountered a mantis on the trail.

"You won your bet," Sir Rudy said to Rufus. "Put it on my bill."

"You can be sure I will, Sir. I hope you don't get curious about anything else that's personal. I can't claim ignorance again."

"Agreed. I admit, it was amusing watching you apologize. You're very good at groveling, aren't you?"

Sir Rudy laughed and Rufus laughed with him. Gabriel thought that Rufus was indeed good at groveling. But then, when one was in his or Rufus' position, one had to be good at it. Those like Sir Rudy would never understand some things. They were used to getting what they wanted and demanding things of those under them. That was the way it went in Roacheria. Gabriel had a private fantasy in which he was the one in control. He made a vow to himself that if it ever came to be, he would treat those beneath him with courtesy.

They were well into the ruins area by this time, with its low bushes and meadow grass. The day had started out clear, but gradually, it clouded over and a cold north wind began to blow. They moved more quickly to keep their muscles and joints from stiffening. The group stopped for a brief rest when they reached the very center of the ruins where the remains of most of the tallest edifices stood.

"Why do you suppose no grassfronds grow here?" Herbert asked.

"I have no idea," Henry said. "No wonder the roaches want so much food from us; this place is so bleak."

"Hoppers would do well here," commented Howard. "But one can't make a steady diet of hoppers. What's life without grassfronds?"

The others nodded their agreement. Grassfronds provided ants with many things: food and oil from the seed, ale from a sour mash made from the seeds, baskets woven from newly sprouted shoots, and many things from the pole-like stems after the seeds were harvested in the fall.

"But why don't they grow here?" persisted Herbert.

"This is far from scientific," said Howard, "merely the opinion of an old ant who knows little, but I think The Creative Essence of the planet cursed this surface when the Duo Pods vanished. Oh, I know what the archaeologists say, that they don't know why the Duo Pods died out, and that's why they still want to keep searching here for answers. Maybe they're right, but then again, maybe they're not. Look at all the things those creatures could do. I'm sure the Duo Pods were as intelligent as we are. They made a lot more things than we do, and we have yet to figure out most of what they left behind. I think they were dangerous. Look at what happened to South Dairy Colony 50 because of some of the toxins they left behind. I think The Essence had had enough and cursed them. Then the planet took its own course again and its care was left to creatures with more respect for the natural order of things."

"It's an interesting thought," Henry said.

They rose to continue their journey. Rufus asked Howard to repeat what he had been talking about, if it wasn't personal. Sir Rudy had taken an interest from the tone of their voices. When it was related, Sir Rudy smiled and said his thanks.

After Rufus finished, Gabriel asked him, "If the customs of Last Day aren't personal, would they tell me a little about that?"

Howard agreed and the two of them discussed it through Rufus for half an h-unit.

The trail continued on through smaller piles of rubble and an occasional tall structure. Ahead of them, Henry could see a long row of bushes, dense with vines and foliage that remained green even in winter.

"What was that, Rufus?" asked Howard.

"What?"

"I thought I heard a noise from near those bushes. Is there a mantis about?"

"No, this area is very safe. You must be imagining it, or maybe there are some crickets. We saw some on secondday."

"Well, I'll feel better when we see those escort warriors you mentioned."

He had no more than finished the sentence when a series of terrifying screams came from the bushes. With the speed of a summer storm, the band of renegades poured from behind the hedge.

Sir Rudy dashed wildly up the trail shouting.

The others stood rooted to the ground, too surprised and afraid to move. With a cruel vengeance, four of the warriors chased Sir Rudy down and tore him to bits. The others and their leader stood in a ring about Rufus, Gabriel, and the ants. Rufus and Gabriel prostrated themselves, saying things in a desperate tone that Henry could not understand.

Rufus shouted at them. "Get down! Humble yourselves if you wish to live!"

Henry, Herbert, and Howard mimicked the position of the two roaches, lying flat on the ground, spreading out their appendages in total helplessness. The renegade warriors were at least two f-units longer and nearly three times as wide as they. Their outer mandibles were opened threateningly. In one lunge they could sever an appendage, crippling their opponent, or decapitate an ant.

Their leader addressed Rufus and Gabriel. Rufus' voice shook as he answered. Henry raised up silent thoughts in meditation, vowing that if he lived, he would never leave the safety of the colony again. He watched in horror as the warriors lifted the part of Gabriel's exoskeleton at the back of his head and passed a line of hemp under it and about his head. They tied the line, then did the same to Rufus.

Rufus turned to them, barely able to speak. "Submit. They won't kill us if we come with them quietly."

Henry and the others remained on the ground, afraid to move. Hemp lines were tied about the slender joints which connected their heads and thoraxes.

"Henry and Herbert," Howard whispered, "keep the line slack. One jerk and you will be decapitated."

Henry followed obediently. He saw Gabriel glance at him, terror in his eyes, as they were led past the pieces of Sir Rudy littering the ground. With shouts of laughter, the warriors picked up Sir Rudy's ornaments and hung them around their own heads.

Henry fought off a wave of nausea. Before he could breathe easily, a second, much larger horde of warriors thundered toward them. Henry had enough presence of mind to grab at the line around his neck and bring in a bit of slack.

Rufus said something to Gabriel and turned to them. "Quick, get between Gabriel and me. Get down! We will try to protect you with our bodies."

A fierce battle raged around them. Screams pierced the air. Roach warriors lunged at the renegades. Mandibles snapped at the main support joint of middle or back legs. A severed pod fell less than an f-unit from where Henry's eyes peeked in dread from beneath Gabriel's abdomen. He felt Gabriel pulling in the lines that connected them together. Gabriel said something. Though his voice shook in fright, Henry thought he was trying to reassure them.

It seemed to go on forever, but finally cries of victory rang out. Henry wondered who had won, and whose prisoners they were now. He didn't have to wait long. Rufus rose and said to them, "Don't be afraid. You can get up now. These are Sir Rudy's warriors, sent by his son to protect us."

The three ants rose uncertainly and looked at the carnage around them. Henry gave in to his nausea. Howard and Herbert closed their eyes and sank to the ground. They sat in the midst of at least twenty mangled bodies. All of the renegades, except their leader, and several of Sir Rudy's warriors lay dead.

"Drink a little water," Rufus said, handing Henry a flask. "Breathe deeply." They waited patiently while a warrior removed the hemp line tying them together. Gabriel put out a pod to help him up. To add to their misery, sky water began falling and the wind grew colder.

Three of the warriors headed back down the trail to collect the remains of Sir Rudy. The leader of the first group yelled as other warriors pinned him down and tied him with his own line. He continued screaming as they dragged him off.

The other leader approached with Rufus. "This is Ganton," Rufus said. "He is chief of Sir Rudy's personal warriors. He says they got word yesterday of a possible attack and have been sitting up in that ruin, watching for us to return. They began to run toward us when they saw the first movement, but were too far away. He is mortified at what happened and says that justice will be dealt out to the renegade leader. We must go quickly with them now to a safe place which has been prepared for you. He wants you to climb onto the backs of some of the warriors because they can run faster than you can. He fears there may be other renegades in the area."

"Who would do such a thing?" Howard asked.

"Many are jealous of Sir Rudy," replied Rufus. "For he is... was a powerful Board Member. I heard one of them mention a name, but I don't have time to go into it now. They will get it out of the one they took prisoner. Be assured of that."

Henry was beyond words. Shaking, he climbed onto the broad back of one of the warriors. The group left the trail and traveled at top speed through open meadows.

Everything seemed strange to Henry, and the more he tried to sort things out, the worse it got. He gave up trying to think. He glanced toward his friends clinging to the backs of other warriors. They looked as dazed as he felt. Ahead, he saw a large area of open earth, full of ruts and gullies, like a scar in the surface. He wondered what it could possibly be and then realized that the ugly place was their destination.

They drew closer. Ganton began shouting to other roaches who scrambled about in response. They whisked around the rim of the pit toward a ruin on the far side. When they reached it, the warriors carrying them stopped.

"Get off and come with me," Rufus said. "They have made a place for you inside this ruin, where no renegade can possibly harm you."

Cold, damp, and still very frightened, they followed without question. Rufus walked behind them and Gabriel followed. One of the warriors led the way down a slope, through a square shaped, synthetic stone tunnel. The warrior gestured for them to enter a lighted chamber at the end.

The ants looked around in dismay. Gabriel's mandibles opened in disgust. The chamber was about fifteen by twenty f-units. Three plain, flat wood surfaces lined one wall, with a lightning bug lamp on each, and a stool in front. A container of parchment sat on the floor beside one of them. Three red floor cushions lined a second wall. A long shelf ran along the third wall. A body waste pot with a basin of water next to it stood in one corner. An eating surface with three more stools stood in the center. A container of drinking water and three mugs sat on top of it. The winter's dampness permeated everything.

"Perhaps," Rufus stammered, "in the haste of the last few days... and then hearing of a possible attack... he hasn't been able to finish it."

"These are the living quarters you spoke of?" Howard asked.

"Well, I was only told about them.. . . I mean, I hadn't seen it. I'm sure this is not complete. I'm sorry, but I must leave you now. You will be safe here from any further attack. I will have food sent to you shortly. I must report all of this to Sir Rudy's son. Everything is such a mess ... His father killed and all ... and you . . . here . . . This isn't the way it was supposed to be."

He backed out slowly and motioned for Gabriel to go with him. The warrior closed the portal.

Howard sighed. "I'm sure it will get better, as Rufus said. At least we're safe. We might as well arrange our things."

Henry had no comment. He was glad to be inside something. Methodically, he took his satchels from his back, opened them, and began to set his manuscripts on one of the surfaces. A few moments later, a warrior entered and set a tray of roasted seeds on the eating surface. He gestured for them to eat. They did and then curled up together on one of the floor cushions--shocked, confused, and exhausted.

10.

*R*ex paced angrily back and forth in front of Ganton, Rufus, and Gabriel. "You stand here telling me my father has been brutally murdered! You couldn't reach him in time! You have three engineers but no tunnel liquid! And I'm not supposed to be upset? Have maggots eaten your brains?" He continued with a long string of curses, picked up a finely crafted pottery figurine, and threw it forcefully to the floor. Rufus cringed.

Ganton prostrated himself before Rex. "I assume full responsibility, Sir. Condemn me if you must. I failed your father and you in my duty."

Rex turned his back to them, and groaned, then changed his tone. "Ganton, I do not blame you for this. You probably did your best under the circumstances. Where are the remains of my father?"

"What we could find, and his ornaments, are in a covered basket in my personal quarters. I will swear to you the same oath I did for your father, if that is your wish."

"It is," said Rex. "I want you always with me over these next time frames as we do what must be done. I should have taken the information from that little spy more seriously. I should have had you meet my father at the border bridge, no matter what he said. Is there any good in this mess?"

"Sir,"   Rufus hesitated, "all is not lost. In the midst of the confusion, I'm certain I heard one of the renegades say, 'Here's to Sir Rollo and his credit.' Also, the agreement worked out with the ants is very good. May I explain?"

Rex drank a full mug of ale, took several deep breaths and sighed. "All right, Rufus. I'm listening."

They talked for over an h-unit. Rufus and Gabriel went over the details of the agreement, why they did not have the tunnel liquid, and their stay with the ants.

"If this is what my father wanted, I'll make the best of it. We will carry it out as he would have. You and Gabriel may leave now. Take tomorrow morning off. Meet with the ants by noon and show them the mine and what we want done. Try to make some sort of long range plan. I won't be with you much for at least a time frame, for obvious reasons."

"Sir, since you will be withdrawn in grief, do you want me to get a few more things for the their quarters?" Rufus asked.

"Why? What's wrong with their quarters?"

"Uh . . . it's a bit cold and damp, rather drab."

"What do they expect?" Rex snapped.

"Not a lot, Sir, but perhaps some coverlets, and a wood burning heat unit."

"Impossible! There's no way to vent a wood burner. I've spent all I'm going to on them. Have the guards bring them hot water once a day in an insulated vat. That's all. Now go and do the job you were hired to do. I'll expect you to testify about what you heard when the Court of Inquiry meets to condemn my father's murderers."

Rufus and Gabriel rose in silence, stooped low and swept their front pods out to the sides as they left.

Walking away from the administration structure, Gabriel said, "Rufus, I know he's upset and grieving. I know I would, if I were he, but those quarters are horrid. Would you want to live there?"

"No, but I tried. You heard him. We can't do anything about it."

"Yes, I can. I'm going home to tell my mate what's happened. Then I'm going to the market and get several coverlets, and a small, portable heat unit and vent pipes. I know how to vent it. We were well treated as their guests. I can't work with them every day and do nothing, no matter what he says."

"If you want to waste your credit and get stepped on, that's your affair. Leave me out of it."

*   *   *   *

Rex's front pods shook, but with relief at how things had turned out, rather than in sadness. "Ganton, take me to what is left of my father. Help me take him home. How will I ever explain this to my sisters? They are only nymphs. Our mother died of an infection not half a season cycle ago. They still weep for her. What will I tell them now? How will I have time to raise them properly, avenge my father, and still run everything here? My father trusted you the most . . . I need you now."

Ganton bowed humbly to his new master. "To you I pledge my loyalty. I will protect you with my own life if need be. I swear to you that I will take to my own covering place anything you tell me in private. Your wishes are above anything of my own. If I fail, may I be condemned to a most horrible death."

Rex accepted Ganton's oath by placing his front pods on the back of Ganton's head. Ganton rose and looked at Rex with complete respect. "I will also testify that I heard Sir Rollo's name mentioned. I will go to the authorities before this day is through, check on that miserable renegade I sent them, and begin the inquiry. We will take your father home now. I will remove his ornaments for you and seal the basket. No one should see him this way. I'll arrange for a covering place near your mother's. I will explain to your sisters. You stay at your home. Many will come to show their loyalty and respect. In private, I will let you know whom you can trust. I will send the fastest messengers to your Uncle Royal, in Sea Edge, and bring him here to help you establish yourself in your father's place."

*   *   *   *

The ants did not awaken until the next morning when two warriors banged open the portal and dragged in a large vat filled with steaming water on a flat roller cart. A third followed with a tray of food. The steam circulated quickly, and was welcomed by the ants, who's joints were stiff with cold. The warriors left, slamming the portal once more. The ants rose slowly.

Herbert looked at the food. "What is this?"

Howard picked up a thin, crisp translucent slice and said, "I think this is what they call fried bees wings."

Herbert made a strange face.

"Our foods probably seem strange to them as well, and I'm too hungry to be particular," Henry said, biting into one.

"I wish we had some herbs for tea," Howard commented. "We'll have to ask Rufus for some when he returns. Meanwhile, we'll settle for warm water." He ladled some from the vat into their mugs.

They had just finished the last of the bees wings when they heard a commotion of voices outside the portal. Amidst the argument, they recognized Gabriel's voice. Before they could wonder much more, the portal opened. Gabriel entered and set down a large bundle. Two skinny workers followed him, carrying several lengths of metal tubing. Two more set down a cylindrical contraption. Gabriel gave the warriors a glare, handed the workers their payment, and turned to smile at the ants. The warriors slammed the portal shut.

Speaking with gestures, Gabriel began to unpack the bundle. First, he took out three brightly colored coverlets and laid them on the floor cushions. He had purchased the brightest ones he could find, even though they cost a bit more. He was glad, because the vivid blue and yellow pattern brightened up the chamber. Then he took out several pots of liquid pigment and some applicators made of strands of wispy thistledown. He demonstrated his intent by quickly sketching a blossom on the drab synthetic stone walls.

The ants smiled appreciatively.

Gabriel proceeded to draw a sketch of what he intended to do with the pipe and the cylindrical contraption, which was a wood burning heat generator. Gabriel had not seen any heat generators in the ant colony except small ones used for cooking. Later, he realized that temperatures underground were fairly constant. The ants had no need for heat generators.

He paced about the chamber and made several measurements. Taking one length of pipe, he poked at the ceiling in the corners, looking for a place that might crumble more easily. The last corner had a crack, which crumbled when he hit it with the pipe. He smiled, and paced the chamber again, counting his paces.

The ants stared at him. He spoke and gestured, trying to make them understand. Henry looked at the sketch Gabriel had made of the flames, smoke, the pipe, and the contraption, drew a sketch of the smoke entering the pipe, and looked quizzically at Gabriel.

Gabriel nodded and smiled. He drew himself leaving with a pipe and indicated that he would be right back. He banged on the portal and yelled for the warriors to let him out.

"Henry, what in the world is he doing?"

"He's installing vent pipes for this thing. Apparently, it burns wood to make heat, but the smoke has to be able to get out. They must not use thistledown filters."

"Or else it's an inefficient unit," Howard said. "I'm very glad you're with us. You seem to be able to figure out what is going on better than either of us. I think you'll be able to work with him on anything."

"I hope so," replied Henry.

They heard muffled banging above them. After quite some time, Gabriel managed to chip a hole in the synthetic stone large enough to force the pipe through. He returned to their chamber and began to connect the pipes together. Henry joined him, following his gestured instructions.

Howard and Herbert picked up the pigment pots and began to decorate the walls with images of blossoms and wood plants.

Rufus stared at them in total amazement when he arrived at noon. "Gabriel, what have you done?"

"What I told you I was going to do."

"You're crazy!"

"But you must admit, it's better."

"Yes, it is." He turned to the ants and spoke in their language. "I can see it's been a busy morning. I'm to take you to the mine. Sir Rudy's son, in spite of his grief, would like us to get started with an inspection and try to form a long-range plan."

Howard said, "The sooner we start, the sooner we'll finish and go home."

"Why do so many guards have to go with us?" Henry asked, as several of them surrounded the group.

"To protect you, of course," replied Rufus. "Sir Rudy's son doesn't want anything to happen to you."

They walked in silence to the rim of the pit. Looking at it more critically now than he had in the confusion and fear of the previous day, Howard said, "Why do you leave this place such a mess? Look at it! It's full of ruts and gullies. The surface here is totally destroyed. There are no plants to prevent a wash out during heavy sky water. That's very dangerous! When we mine an area, you don't even know it's there. As one place is mined out, its tunnels are filled with diggings from new areas. The surface remains in its natural state."

Rufus gave him a confused look. "This is the way we've always done things. It would be very expensive to fill in this surface. Prices would rise even more."

"Well, it should be done," Howard persisted. "This is an inexcusable wrong against Essence. When you take too much from the natural order of things, cycles can be broken. Every creature in the interdependent chain of life suffers."

Rufus shifted uneasily. "In your philosophy, yes. I'll share your concern with Sir Rudy's son, and try to explain your ways to him."

They picked their way down the slope and through the mud left by the previous day's sky water. Rufus explained to Gabriel what Howard had said. They were still talking when the group reached the tunnel entrance. The three ants climbed all around it, poking at the soil, testing the conditions. Howard dug a small amount from the rubble in the entrance.

"How many f-units collapsed?" Howard asked.

Rufus related the question to Gabriel and translated his responses. "Gabriel says about sixty f-units collapsed. Nothing has been done since it happened. He wants you to know that as we clear it, we may find some of those who died. He wants you to be prepared for that. It may not be pleasant. I will have our workers ready with covered body baskets."

Howard nodded. "The soil is very soft. This will be an easy repair. We may finish in less than six time frames, but we must work with caution. Soft soil shifts easily. I noticed a lot of clay in the soil as we came down the slope. We should reinforce the tunnel walls with some of it. As we do that, we can teach you how to prepare the surface for new plant life, so this place can rejuvenate itself."

They did more soil testing, and further explained about the clay. Gabriel was very attentive to all the description, and said he would like to return to their chamber so he could use parchment more easily and make drawings.

The ant's quarters were cozy and dry from the wood burner when they returned. They worked in comfort until supper. Gabriel was almost sorry that the day was over. "Rufus, teach me to say 'thank you' in Ant. And how should I gesture to them?"

That first evening, his words sounded strange. As the ants took both his front pods in a friendly greeting, he let go and stooped low. The ants accepted his awkward effort with appreciative smiles.

*   *   *   *

Except for the two h-units Ganton had spent at the Detention Facility reporting to the enforcers and beginning the Formal Inquiry, he had not left Rex's side. At night, he had slept on a pallet outside Rex's portal, and he had posted several guards outside Rex's residence, and under the window. All seventhday, Ganton sat quietly in the main parlor next to Rex and the sealed basket which contained Sir Rudy, as Board Members and prominent citizens of Roacheria came and went, expressing their dismay about what had happened, promising the same loyalty to Rex that they had given Sir Rudy.

The comments were all the same. "I'm shocked!" "Have The Enforcers detained anyone yet?" "Who woud dare to do such a thing?" Rex was bored to the breaking point, but his blank expression only reinforced his "grief" in the eyes of his visitors.

Relief came when his Uncle Royal arrived seventhday evening. Royal had not been to visit since Rex had finished training four season cycles before. Rex liked his uncle, who was Supreme Executor of The Board in Sea Edge. He controlled everyone there the way Rex hoped to control the South East Roach Control Board, which had more power than the Sea Edge's local board.

Royal embraced him formally. "Rex, I wish I were here under different circumstances. The last few season cycles your father has been overconfident and careless."

"It's truly good to see you, Uncle Royal. Let's move into my father's private parlor."

Ganton followed. When they were comfortable and had been served plenty of food, Ganton said, "Sir Royal, I've made a list of everyone who came today, and those should have come and didn't."

"Good! Rex, you hang on to this one. He was your father's right-front pod. Unfortunately, Rudy didn't listen well enough to his advice. I hope you are wiser."

Rex nodded. They went over the list carefully, discussing who could be trusted, bought off, or intimidated into submission, and formed both short term and long range plans.

"Ganton, how's the inquiry coming?" Royal asked.

"That stupid renegade couldn't confess fast enough about who hired him. The Enforcers took Sir Rollo to the Detention Facility sixthday morning. I was told he's insisting he's innocent. Can you imagine the nerve? Both Rufus and I heard his name mentioned. Plus, they actually found a satchel of credit notes with Sir Rollo's name in it at the precise place the renegade said it would be."

"How long before The Inquiry makes its judgment?"

"It should be immediately, but you know how it is. He'll have good counselors. They'll manage to drag it out a couple of time frames accusing everyone else they can think of," Ganton replied.

"Rex, it's going to get ugly," Royal said. "Rollo's counselors may even accuse you, trying to prove his innocence. After the covering tomorrow, why don't you let me take Regina and Rolinda back to Sea Edge with me? They need female guidance right now to prepare them for their proper place in the establishment. My mate suggested it before I left. You don't need the strain of supervising them with everything else."

Rex sighed. "Thank you. I'll send a living allowance from my father's assets every time frame."

"My mate will find the best tutors available. If I don't use all you send, I'll put it in trust toward their future mating contracts. Be sure you keep any other assets your father intended for them for that purpose. The more the assets, the more choosy we can be in finding proper mates for them when they come of age."

Rex thanked him and complained that he was tired. He said good night and entered the seclusion of his sleep chamber where he poured himself a mug of ale and celebrated his private victory. Except for tunnel liquid, things were going exactly as he had planned.

11.

*A*deline went about her life, trying not to think about the empty evenings and how incredibly lonely she felt. Each night's entry in her journal seemed the same: the same daily routine, the same count down of days, less one, the same statements about how much she missed Henry. She longed for the end of the first time frame, when the traders would bring the regular plastic shipment from Roacheria and expected letters from Henry in exchange for processed grasshopper, grassfrond seeds and other produce. She had a stack of letters to send.

She appreciated Deanna more than ever. Even though she had often comforted her sister, she had not realized how Deanna actually felt. She reminded herself that for her it would end and Henry would return.

At the end of the third quarter time frame, Deanna came to her chamber in the evening. "Adeline, I'm sorry to interrupt your letter writing, but Alyssa is here."

Adeline rose and followed her sister. "Alyssa, it's good to see you. What brings you here?"

Alyssa took Adeline's front pods in greeting. "I don't want to worry you, but we got some information from the Intercolonial Council today. Right after Henry, Herbert, and Howard left, we sent copies of the agreement with Sir Rudy, so I.C. would know of our attempt to improve relations with Roacheria."

"Is something wrong?"

"They said everything seemed to be in order, but they had some upsetting news concerning the interpreter, Rufus. They had reports from three other colonies on the northern border with Roacheria. He went to each colony on behalf of the South East Roach Control Board to negotiate new trading arrangements. Afterward, each colony found out that there were differences in the copies of the agreements. They found themselves obligated to send twice as much of our goods for half as much plastic."

Adeline's mandibles opened in shock. "What did they do about it?"

"The colony councils contacted the S.E.R.C.B. to find the source of the error. Each was told the same thing; that our councils should have been more attentive to the details. The roaches said they couldn't help it if we didn't notice that a numerical point was misplaced. The councils decided they had to abide by their agreements, but vowed to be more cautious if Rufus ever returned there."

Adeline looked at her in dismay. "What's wrong with our contract?"

"Hopefully, nothing. The Intercolonial Council said that since Sir Rudy came here in person, and they know he is an important Board Member, it was less likely that Rufus would make errors. In the other cases, Rufus had negotiated the deals by himself. The Intercolonial Council wants us to keep in close contact as time goes on. When you get your first letters from Henry, would you mind passing on any information? I've already talked to Herbert's family and Howard's daughter. That's why I arrived here so late."

"Of course. I'll bring you the letters after I've read them."

"Oh, goodness, no, I wouldn't dream of asking you to share personal communications. Just let me know if he's being treated well and if anything seems to be wrong with the amount of funds."

*   *   *   *

The first several days of tunneling had been difficult for the three ants. None of the poorly trained mine workers knew how to read.

Rufus laughed it off. "Not everyone wants to learn, you know. Some of these workers couldn't anyway. They never got enough plastic during nymphhood."

"Why not?" Herbert asked.

"Well, you can feed your larvae as you please. They accept anything you give them, and your pupas don't even know they're being fed, but nymphs are different. If they get stubborn and refuse to eat, there's not a lot a parent can do. I'm constantly telling my son, 'Eat your plastic like a good nymph. Do you want to grow up to be stupid?' Sometimes he listens, sometimes he doesn't."

Gabriel looked at Rufus and asked him what he had said. "Why didn't you say that the families of these workers can't afford enough plastic?" he retorted.

"Because they would find it offensive," Rufus snapped.

Rufus had very little knowledge about tunnels. Howard had to explain all the procedures to Rufus, show him what to do, and then wait while he tried to explain it to Gabriel and the workers. The slow process tried their patience.

More than once, Herbert said, "Why don't we send them home and do it ourselves. It would be much faster."

However, they all knew that the whole point was to teach the roaches. As Gabriel began to understand the general ideas, he was more effective in directing the workers. By the second quarter time frame, Rufus got better at explaining things.

At the end of the third quarter time frame, they had a good system going. Howard told Rufus what to do and he directed the workers. Herbert demonstrated what they needed to do and worked alongside the roaches. His gestures and actual work were worth a thousand words. The roach workers began to copy his actions as they listened to Rufus.

"These workers aren't suffering from Plastic Deprivation. I don't think you creatures give them proper training," Howard said to Rufus.

Rufus just twitched his antennae.

Most of the time, Henry stayed with Gabriel with a flat slate, parchment, and ink, sketching, and showing him the calculations; then having Gabriel do the same thing himself. When the first time frame ended, they had cleared and rebuilt twenty f-units of the collapsed tunnel. They had also recovered ten bodies.

Gabriel often stayed into the evening, sitting with Henry in the ants' quarters, watching attentively, as they drew diagrams for the next day. The warriors got used to Gabriel's presence, often leaving the portal open when he was there, but watching closely. The ants accepted being locked in, since Rufus constantly told them horror stories of bandits who roamed about the mine area at night trying to scavenge plastic illegally.

Rufus attended to their physical needs. They had plenty of food, water, and occasionally tea. Rufus explained that Roaches did not drink much tea. It was hard to find the right herbs at the market. The ants got used to unfamiliar foods.

A few days before the end of the first time frame, Henry handed Rufus a stack of letters. "Would you see that these are given to the traders before their scheduled trip?"

"All for Adeline?"

Henry shook his head. "I have a family, and so do Howard and Herbert."

"I'm sorry, no offense meant. I'll take them to the trade center myself, and pick up any letters for you."

*   *   *   *

Rufus went straight to Rex's work chamber.

"Is he seeing anyone yet?" he asked the female worker sitting outside the portal. For the first several days, only Ganton had been admitted to what had formerly been Sir Rudy's work chamber. Lately, Rufus hadn't needed to see Sir Rex.

"Yes, I'll tell him you're here."

A moment later, Rufus was told to go in.

"Good afternoon, Sir," Rufus said, stooping and sweeping his front pods outward.

"Sit down, Rufus. How are things going? I've watched from the rim a time or two."

Rufus hoped he would be offered refreshments, but he wasn't. "Things have smoothed out, Sir. I have their first batch of letters. What do you want me to do with them?" He placed the pile on Rex's work surface.

Rex glanced through the pile. "Why are there so many with this same script?" He pointed to one of Henry's to Adeline.

"Those are Henry's. They're to his Promised One."

"What?"

Once again, Rufus found himself trying to explain something that really didn't translate into Roach. "I tried to tell your father that taking one who is promised is like taking one who is mated. I told him it would cause problems, but he was determined to have that engineer. He really is very talented, Sir, the best of the three."

Rex shook his head in disgust. He looked at Rufus curiously. "I wonder what he says in his letters. Read one of them to me."

Rufus broke the seal on one and glanced over it. "It says, 'My cherished Adeline, Things have gotten a little better since we first arrived. I wrote you about how Gabriel brought the heat unit and other things in the beginning that make this wretched chamber more tolerable. Truly, if it weren't for him, I think I would try to leave immediately. He is eager to learn, and very intelligent. I'm not sure I would do as well if I were trying to learn this in another language. Yesterday marked our second seventhday here. We meditated together for quite some time. I concentrated my thoughts on you. I long for you so much that sometimes when I dream of you at night, I awaken thinking I'll find you near me. Perhaps if we both meditate at exactly the same time, my essence might touch yours and we can comfort each other. I look forward to your reply to this. There are 150 days until I see you again. Your Henry.' That's it for this one, Sir."

"What does he mean about Gabriel putting in a heat unit?"

"Well, Sir," Rufus shifted uneasily, since he had not told Rex about it before. "That first day, Gabriel took it upon himself to fix up their quarters." He explained about the pigments, the coverlets, and the vent pipes, assuring Rex that the ants could not escape through the vents.

"Gabriel is crazy, but I need him."

"That's what I told him, Sir."

Rex laughed. "Meditate . . . his essence might touch hers . . . I always knew ants were demented. Do not deliver these letters. We need to cut all contact. When they ask where their letters are, make up something. You're good at that. If South Harvester 45 should ask why these three haven't sent anything, make up a good lie for them, too. I'll keep these. I wonder what the communications department would pay for them so that trainees would have something to practice translating. Be sure you bring me anything that comes from South Harvester 45."

"Of course, Sir."

"And don't mention this to Gabriel. Oh, here, I nearly forgot. Translate this and give it to them. It's their first time frame's expense report."

Rufus glanced down the list. The prices charged were about ten times the actual amounts. "Sir, at this rate, they'll end up owing you credit."

"It was your suggestion. That's how I'll justify keeping them here."

*   *   *   *

"Rufus, this can't possibly be correct," Howard said, staring at the expense statement.

Rufus shifted. "Let me check it again." He went over the figures. "I'm afraid it is, Howard. I don't set the prices. I just had the things you wanted delivered to you."

"Are these the amounts everyone here pays?" asked Henry incredulously.

"Yes, basics are expensive here."

"Why didn't you say so before we came?" Herbert asked.

"You didn't ask. We discussed living expenses. Surely you remember that. The delivery charges are higher because of the bandit problem. We couldn't anticipate that. Perhaps you could do with less. I would take more time now, but I can't. Please, excuse me." He glanced at his time piece. "I'm late for an appointment." He called to the guards and was let out.

"Well," said Henry, "it certainly tells us why the amount offered seemed so high." He made some quick calculations. "We'd better figure out what we can do without, or we will owe them in six time frames."

Together, they went over the list. They gave up tea, cut back on grasshopper meat, and some other things that came from South Harvester 45, and rationalized that as the weather warmed, they would no longer need the wood burner.

When all the difficult decisions had been made, Herbert said, "I wonder what else we should have asked them more about."

"Cheer up," said Howard. "Tomorrow we'll have letters."

*   *   *   *

Gabriel sat with the ants late the next evening. He and Henry communicated quite well with gestures and drawings. Gabriel often asked the names of things in Ant and would repeat them until he remembered. Common greetings such as, "Good morning", "Good night", and, "How are you?" came easily. Since he was learning tunnel terminology for the first time, he learned it correctly in Ant. They had about finished the next day's plan when Rufus arrived, breathless.

"Rufus, what's wrong?" Howard asked.

"I'm afraid I have very bad news. I've just come from the trade center. The place was bedlam. Bandits attacked the traders returning from South Harvester 45. They opened every sealed parchment, looking for credit, I guess. When there was none, because special envoys are sent to carry credit, and they are heavily guarded, they became angry and tore every bit of parchment to shreds! All the letters I hoped to give you this evening were destroyed."

"Surely, there must be something," said Henry.

"No, they had nothing for me. But yours were sent. They said there were no problems on the trip to your colony."

"At least they'll have word from us," Herbert said, trying to be cheerful.

"I'm very sorry," Rufus said, hanging his head low and drooping his antennae. "Gabriel, we'd better go. It's getting late."

The portal banged shut behind the two roaches and they headed home. Gabriel asked what he had told the ants. When Rufus told him, Gabriel snapped, "You liar! There was no bandit attack. Where are their letters?"

Rufus looked directly into Gabriel's eyes and said with complete sincerity, "There really weren't any. I don't know if they missed the traders or what, but I decided it would be easier to say that. How would you feel if you were they, and after all this time, there were no letters? Wouldn't you rather think they were destroyed, than know that there weren't any?"

Gabriel said nothing.

*   *   *   *

Adeline stood in front of the chief receiving ant in the communications department, almost in tears. "What do you mean, there were no letters? I know Henry would write to me."

"Adeline, I don't know what went wrong. But there were no communications from Roacheria this trip, not even official ones. The traders didn't have an interpreter with them, but from their gestures, we understood that they had left very early in the morning. Perhaps those who were to give letters to the traders did not arrive before the traders left. Maybe they will send another special envoy with all the formal communications. I'll have someone bring letters right to your domicile if that happens." He put his front pod on the back of her thorax in comfort.

"Thank you," she said, and turned to leave.

*   *   *   *

Rex laughed loudly at the sentimental lines in the letters from South Harvester 45, as Rufus translated them. "Are they really all that caring, Rufus? I mean, all the time?"

Rufus twitched his antennae. "Yes, Sir, that's how they are."

"Keep up the good work. Here's the bonus I've been promising you for your silence about certain matters," Rex said, handing Rufus a pod full of plastic exchange notes.

"At your service, as always, Sir," Rufus said, backing out humbly.

Later, Rex took both sets of letters to the Communications Training Center and sold them for a tidy sum.

12.

*T*he ants worked at a feverish pace for the next several days, reasoning that they would finish the job as quickly as possible and put Roacheria behind them. Half way through the second time frame, they removed the last of the debris from the collapse.

Their eyes met a gruesome sight and a stench enveloped them. Sprawled about, lay the last of the roach workers who had been caught inside the mine when the tunnel collapsed. Until that moment, Gabriel thought that everyone had been buried by falling debris. Now, it was evident that some had survived the cave in, but had been trapped with no food or water.

Gabriel sank to the ground. "I am worse than pond scum. They might have been saved."

"No, Gabriel," Rufus tried to reassure him. "Even if the digging had begun the day it happened, they would still have died for lack of water." He repeated Gabriel's statement and his response in Ant.

"What an awful death they suffered," Howard said quietly. "The others, at least, went quickly. Such a waste. So preventable. Why didn't you come to us for help to build your tunnels long ago?"

Rufus beckoned to the roach workers to bring body baskets and then led Gabriel and the ants outside for some fresh air. An h-unit later, Howard, Henry, and Herbert stood at the end of their newly built section and looked at the roach tunnel.

"This whole thing is a death trap. Look at the ceiling. I'm amazed it's still holding. This timber is badly cracked and rotted," Howard said, pointing to the closest support timber. He turned to Rufus. "The only way we can repair this tunnel is to pull a controlled collapse, let it settle and start from the beginning. How many f-units to the actual mining area?"

Rufus relayed the question to Gabriel. Gabriel's antennae drooped in shame. "I tried and tried to get Sir Rudy to do this right. He wouldn't listen to me. It's about two-hundred f-units to the production area. What you did there," he said, pointing to the part they had finished, "is excellent work. Please, keep teaching me how to do this. What must I do to help you with this next part?"

Howard held the lamp high and cautiously walked down the tunnel to a place ahead where it curved. He disappeared around the curve momentarily and returned. "We need to run a strong line of hemp right to the end and tie it to a support timber, bring it back here where we will be safe, and pull the timber out. When it settles, we tie another line to the next one that's still standing and do the same until it's all caved in. It should settle for two days before excavation begins again."

"How long will it take?" Rufus asked. "Sir Rudy's son will want to know and approve this plan, since it means further delay in production."

Howard's sharp voice cut in, "You tell him he'd better accept it, because I'll leave tonight if he doesn't! If he wants his tunnel, we do it my way. I signed an agreement to build a safe tunnel and I won't do any less. I refuse to let any work I leave behind me endanger any creature, ant or roach. My essence will never rest if there is the possibility of causing anyone's death in the way that I saw today. We will finish it within six time frames as we agreed to do. And by the way, what is Sir Rudy's son's name? When will we ever meet him?"

Howard's bluntness caught Rufus off guard. "Uh . . . I . . . I mean Gabriel and I . . . will take this news to him right now . . . We will stop our work until we . . . know his answer. I do not use Sir Rudy's son's name out of respect for Sir Rudy. It is our custom, especially during the formal grieving period. I cannot say for certain when he will come to meet you. I'm sure it will not be until after the Formal Inquiry has condemned Sir Rudy's murderers."

Howard calmed down. "Forgive me, if I have offended you. I spoke harshly in anger and forgot his grief."

"It's all right," Rufus replied. "I know there have been many times I offended you."

*   *   *   *

The ants returned to their quarters and Rufus and Gabriel headed for Rex's work chamber. On the way, Rufus repeated the conversation he had had with Howard.

There was a hint of sarcasm in Gabriel's voice. "Watch out, Rufus, you might start to imitate them and tell the truth more often. I might even get to like you."

Rufus stopped. "It won't be easy to convince him that this plan is best. Humble yourself and back me up. We both need our jobs." They walked the rest of the way in silence.

The attendant motioned for them to go in. Both roaches bowed respectfully. Rex sat quietly as they related the events of the morning. He glared at them. "So?"

Gabriel began. "What they want to do now is to collapse the rest of the tunnel and start all over. I'm beginning to learn their methods, Sir. This really would be the best way for me to learn. Your father's intent was that I should learn and be able to teach others. That is the agreement I signed with him and you. They assure me we will complete it within the agreed upon time."

Rex tapped his front pod anxiously. "My profits are in the hands of five idiots. I'm supposed to suspend all mining for another four time frames while you play with your tunnels. And who is paying for all this, I might ask?"

Gabriel continued. "Sir, we must do it their way, or not at all. Howard said he would leave and he meant it."

"Oh, he did, did he? They aren't going anywhere, and you can . . ." He stopped short. In his anger, he'd almost said the wrong thing in front of Gabriel.

He paced around the chamber. In his mind, he calculated his reserve supplies and the cost of paying workers without new plastic to sell.

In spite of how he despised both Rufus and Gabriel, he knew he needed them and the ants for his long range goals. After pacing for several minutes, he faced the two again. "What is the lowest number of workers you need to build this tunnel their way?"

Gabriel thought a moment. Sometimes, it seemed like there were too many and they got in the way. "I could pick out ten of the most intelligent and we could do it, Sir."

"All right. You pick your ten and tell the rest there will be no more work until we begin production again. They will be notified when to report back to work. They can pick up this quarter time frame's pay as they leave today."

*   *   *   *

"I'll take the line down and tie it to the farthest support timber," offered Henry the following morning.

"No, Henry, I will," insisted Howard.

"But if something goes wrong. We need your experience, Howard."

"No, I will take the risk. Your lives are before you and, Henry, Adeline is waiting for you. My life is mostly behind me. Rufus, tell the workers they are not to enter the tunnel at all while we do this."

Henry was secretly relieved. He hated to see Howard risk his life, but he had no desire to go down such a dangerous tunnel. They watched him disappear around the curve and lifted up silent thoughts for his safety. A few moments later he returned. The three ants and Gabriel pulled hard on the line. They heard a crack, then a rumbling noise and fled toward daylight.

They waited an h-unit before going back in. Once again, Howard cautiously ventured into the worst area and attached another line. When he returned, he said that their first attempt had collapsed about sixty f-units. As they waited for the second controlled collapse to settle, Howard outlined their work for the next two days.

"Gabriel should spend his time with us going over charts and drawings. He can learn a lot through sketching and practicing the calculations. Henry, would you begin some of the more advanced graphics and equations with him?"

"Of course."

"Herbert, you and I can guide the other workers. We'll get more clay out of these slopes and prepare them so wind blown seeds can take root and rejuvenate this place. Rufus, will you try to explain to Sir Rudy's son that this will make the whole area safer and prevent flood damage when the next severe summer storm hits?"

"Yes, Sir, I will," replied Rufus.

"Call me 'Howard,' not 'Sir'. We work together as equals in this group."

Rufus smiled. "As you wish, Howard."

"Let's finish it."

Howard picked up another length of hemp and headed into the tunnel. As he attached the line to the timber at the curve within their sight, Henry spotted the falling dust.

"Howard, run! It's giving in by itself!"

He had no sooner gotten the words out than the dust turned to chunks of dirt. Rufus and Gabriel were already running way ahead of them. Henry looked for Howard. He had stumbled and fallen. Henry turned to go back for him.

"**No!**" screamed Howard. "Get out of here!"

Henry reluctantly ran down the new part of the tunnel, then stopped. He coughed in the dust but stayed there. He could remember the feeling of a stable tunnel from the times he had repaired his own. Herbert joined him. They waited only a minute after the rumbling stopped. Herbert ran to get another lantern, while Henry started back down the tunnel.

"Howard, where are you?" Henry called, groping his way through the dark. He bent down, let his antennae guide him, and called out again. He heard a weak coughing and crawled toward the sound. "Howard, answer me if you can."

He was rewarded with a weak, "Here."

Henry reached him a moment before Herbert arrived with the lantern. Howard was half buried under medium sized rocks and soil. The two worked frantically, flinging soil behind them with their front and middle pods. They had freed Howard by the time Rufus and Gabriel reached them.

"Ah! My back appendage!" cried Howard as they moved him to a safer spot.

Herbert stooped to look at it. "Rufus, hold that lantern higher, please. Your leg's broken, Howard, but it's a clean break. It's between the joints, and it will heal well in time. We'll bind it right away."

Gabriel spoke to Rufus. "What do they need? Ask them!"

"How can we help?" Rufus said.

"I need some binding material and a straight piece of wood, about like this," said Herbert, using his pods to show them.

Rufus and Gabriel ran off. Henry sat at Howard's head stroking him gently. "I should have yelled sooner."

"No, Henry, I owe you my life. I don't have eyes behind me. You saw the first sign. I would have made it, but I tripped."

They sat in silence, pondering their close call. Rufus and Gabriel returned.

"Will this do?" Rufus asked, handing them a long straight branch he had broken from a small wood plant near the rim of the mine.

"It'll be fine."

Carefully, Henry held Howard's broken back appendage, while Herbert bound the branch to it with strips of woven thistledown. Gabriel handed him more from the emergency kit the ants had placed near the entrance. When they had splinted Howard's appendage as best they could, Herbert brought in one of the dirt hauling baskets. Together, he and Henry gently picked up Howard and laid him in it.

"I'm sorry it's not cushioned, Howard," Herbert said, "but it's the best we can do."

Howard didn't speak. His mandibles were clenched in pain.

Henry reached out and stroked him. "We'll carry it as carefully as we can, so we won't jostle you."

When they came out of the mine, the workers murmured among themselves, as though relieved they had been spared this time.

Henry turned to Rufus. "Please, lead the way to your closest medical facility. It's not a bad break, but it needs to be plastered."

Rufus stammered, "Uh . . . Our surgeons won't know how to treat it. He's not a roach."

Henry stared at him. "Look at your appendage. Look at mine. Are they that different? Look at yourself. Maybe our surgeons didn't do it perfectly in their lack of knowledge of roaches, but you seem to be doing all right. Pardon my rudeness, but I only see one or two crooked scars on your thorax. Herbert and I have both had some emergency training. We've already set and splinted it. All we need is a doctor to do the plastering and some herbs to ease his pain. Now, which way do we go?"

Gabriel guessed the meaning of their conversation and motioned for them to follow him. Rufus stopped him and whispered, "We can't take them to the city. Imagine it. He would condemn both of us."

"We have to do something," Gabriel replied. "If you won't, I will. I'll pay for it myself again, too, if I must."

Rufus turned back to Henry. "It's still not safe to take you there. Renegades may be lurking about the empty areas between this mine and the main part of the city. Take him back to your quarters while I go after a doctor."

The warriors escorted the ants back to their quarters where Herbert and Henry laid Howard on his sleeping cushion. While Herbert fixed some tea, which they now considered a luxury, Henry continued to stroke Howard's antennae.

Rufus and Gabriel headed for Rex's work chamber. Rufus' antennae twitched in anxiety. "How are we going to explain this one? As angry as he was about doing it their way, how do we ask him for a physician?"

"You're such a coward," Gabriel replied. "You think he's all powerful. He gave in yesterday, and he'll give in today for the same reason: he needs us. He can't get what he wants without your translating or my ability to learn this technology. He'll whine and he'll yell, but he'll send a doctor out there. You'll see. I can handle him."

When they arrived at the portal of Rex's work chamber, the female attendant was nowhere in sight. "We'd better wait to make sure he's in," suggested Rufus.

Gabriel didn't hesitate. He tapped three times on the portal and then, without waiting for an answer, turned the latch and entered. A surprised cry came from within. The female attendant's antennae popped up from behind Rex's work surface. She made a hasty retreat back to her work station.

Rex's voice came from behind his work surface. "Where did that cursed piece of parchment go?" In a moment, he rose and looked at them, his face filled with surprise and irritation. Rufus prostrated himself and remained in a submissive position.

Gabriel didn't give Rex time to recover from his embarrassment. He stood as an equal and said calmly, "Sir, there has been an accident, a minor one. The controlled collapse went well until the last section. A timber gave out before we were ready. Howard was caught up in the falling debris. Fortunately, he suffered only a fractured back appendage. The other two ants splinted it and he is resting in their quarters. If you order a doctor out there immediately to plaster it, and give him something for the pain, he could be carried in a cushioned basket and direct the work when we begin to dig the tunnel again. If you don't get it properly treated, he's useless to you and the work will go more slowly."

Rex stared at them, trying to recover his thoughts, then sighed in disgust. He took a piece of parchment, wrote a message on it and handed it to Rufus, who was still on the floor. "Rufus, get up. Take this to my personal physician, who's name and location you see here. He knows how to do things quietly. Stay with him the whole time. Bring him to me when he's finished. Gabriel, you stay here." His voice was calm, but his face now revealed fury.

"Yes, Sir. At once, Sir," Rufus said, rising only enough to take the parchment before he backed out, closing the portal behind him.

Rex turned on Gabriel. With one fast swoop of his back pod, he knocked Gabriel to the floor and pounced on his back. He placed his strongest back pod on the weakest part of the plate behind Gabriel's head and pressed down, pinning the smaller roach helplessly.

"You miserable, insolent piece of fly bait! Don't you ever enter this chamber again without being announced and without the proper humility for your lowly position. You are never to make a demand of me! If you have a legitimate need, you make a humble request, and I, in my position of authority, will decide to grant it, if I find it is truly necessary. Now beg for pardon." He pressed down harder.

Gabriel could not move and could barely breathe. "Forgive me Sir," he whispered. "I am but your lowly servant, no better than the dust beneath your pods. In utter disgrace, I ask you for mercy and beg to be allowed to continue to serve you."

Rex got off his back. Gabriel remained on the floor, gasping.

"That's better," Rex snapped. "Don't you ever forget this lesson. Now get out of here!"

Gabriel did not rise to his full height. He stayed low and backed out without a sound.

*   *   *   *

Over an h-unit passed before Rufus arrived with the Roacherian doctor. Rufus introduced them. "Sir Rudy's son has sent you his own private physician. Please, stand aside and let him work."

The doctor looked around the chamber in disgust. "He'd better make this trip worth my while." He leaned over Howard and examined the splint. "Not a bad job. Who splinted this?"

"They did," Rufus replied, pointing to the ants.

"Tell them they did well. And tell this one to hang onto something. It's not quite straight. It's going to hurt plenty when I reset it. I should do this with the patient asleep, but my sleep inducing apparatus can't be removed from the clinic."

Rufus explained this to the ants. Henry let Howard grip his front pods and braced himself, but Howard passed out as the surgeon cut the binding that held the splint in place. The doctor took advantage of his unconsciousness and worked as quickly as he could to correct the setting and apply the plaster.

"Tell them not to revive him. Let him sleep as long as possible. If he wakes up before the plaster is completely dry, they must restrain him. Any movement before it dries will break the set. They should mix a measure of this mold with liquid and have him drink it once each day for the next seven days to fight infection," he said, taking a container from his satchel and setting it on their eating surface. He set out several packets of dried leaves and bark. "They should put one of these packets in a mug of boiling water and have him drink it every few h-units for pain for the next two or three days. He shouldn't need it after that. When the plaster is hard, he can move about as much as he feels comfortable. I suppose Rex wants him working as soon as possible?"

"Yes, Doctor," Rufus replied.

"They'd better carry him for the next time frame. After that, they can tie the plastered appendage up against his body and he can hobble about on five. Send for me at the end of the second time frame and I'll come back and remove the plaster. Tell Rex he should fix this place up better. Except for those bright coverlets and the images, it's awful. It's worse than some of the shanties. If that sanitation facility isn't sterilized daily, they'll catch some nasty infection when the weather warms in spring."

"Maybe he'll listen to you if you tell him yourself. He wishes to see you before you leave," Rufus said.

Rufus relayed all the doctor's instructions to Herbert and Henry and then left with the doctor. The following day, with warrior escort, Henry and Herbert were permitted to go to the surface, where they dug their own properly constructed body refuse disposal area, well away from their quarters and the mine pit. Roach guards accompanied them whenever they went there.

13.

*G*abriel walked toward the center of the city of Roacheria, where the Justice Building stood next to the edifice which housed the South East Roach Control Board meeting chambers. The Justice Building stood on the foundation of an old Duo Pod ruin, whose lower areas had been converted into the Detention Facility. Above the ground, it was an impressive sight. It was built from pieces of synthetic stone (remnants of Duo Pod buildings) and chunks of mauve-shaded limestone hauled from far away. The two kinds of materials were arranged in a striking pattern on the outside walls. The main portal was made of thick wooden slabs, elaborately carved with images of the important roaches who had formed Organized Roacheria many season cycles before.

The Banner of Organized Roacheria hung from the roof of the Justice Building down onto the upper part of the outside walls. Gabriel looked up at it and thought about the symbolism he had been taught as a nymph. Three arrows pointed inward to the silhouette of a large brown roach in the center. If the arrows had been connected, they would have formed an inverted triangle. The upper arrows were yellow on the right and red on the left. The one pointing upward from the bottom was blue.

All nymphs were taught that these were the primary colors of nature, and that when they were mixed in equal amounts they formed the beautiful brown of a roach's exoskeleton. Nature blended itself to form the superior being, a roach, and the roach was the center of everything.

There was another meaning that was never stated in formal training, or mentioned anywhere in any manuscript. But every roach knew it, especially the poor and those without any formal training. The yellow arrow stood for credit, the red for political power, the blue for those who had neither. The roach in the center stood on those represented by the blue arrow.

Gabriel dragged his pods up the ramp and entered. Rex had given him another painful reminder of the banner's second meaning the evening before. Rex told him bluntly what he was to say when he stood before the Formal Inquiry, which was expected to condemn Sir Rollo and the renegade leader.

Gabriel had not heard any names during the attack. He did not deny that Rufus or Ganton did, but he had been too terrified to pay much attention to anything. Now he was expected to state that he had definitely heard the name mentioned.

Once inside, Gabriel found Rufus and Ganton and joined them. The three entered a large open chamber and took their seats in the area reserved for those expected to testify. Rex was not there yet. He would enter later from a side chamber reserved for victims and their families, and would be seated on a more comfortable bench than those provided for witnesses.

The Chief Enforcer entered from yet another portal at the front. Every roach present stooped low in submission to his authority as he took his place.

"Bring in the guilty parties," said the Chief Enforcer.

Sir Rollo and the renegade were dragged in from the back. Both had now spent nearly two time frames confined in the lower levels of the Justice Structure. They were dirty, smelly, and their exoskeletons were dull from lack of food. At that time, prisoners in Roacheria were kept in horrible conditions, rarely fed or given fresh water, and denied proper sanitary facilities. The Enforcers didn't care if someone accused of a crime died before the Formal Inquiry. It saved the citizens of Roacheria the cost of an inquiry and maintenance of prisoners. Only the most wealthy had help from a professional counselor to try to prove their innocence.

At that point, Rex entered. He seated himself on a cushioned bench and lowered his antennae in grief. Gabriel saw that he was wearing all his father's ornaments in addition to his own.

The Chief Enforcer addressed the renegade. "You are guilty of the murder of Sir Rudy, member of the South East Roach Control Board. I have one question for you. Who paid you to carry out this despicable crime?"

"Sir Rollo did. We met at Bush Row in the early h-units of the third day of this season cycle."

The Chief Enforcer stated his sentence. "You will be taken to the Center for the Condemned immediately. Tomorrow, your mandibles will be cut off by a surgeon without regard to your pain. You will be delivered to the mantis compound the following morning at dawn. May the mantis enjoy its meal, and may you suffer more than your victim. Take him away!"

Sir Rollo's counselor rose from his place and stooped low before the Chief Enforcer. "If it pleases you, Lord Chief Enforcer, may I be granted permission to ask this renegade questions?"

"Yes, you may," the Chief Enforcer replied.

The counselor addressed the renegade. "Bush Row is thick with vines. How could you see who was speaking to you? In the dead of night, how could you be so certain of your employer?"

"I am well acquainted with Sir Rollo. I have seen him often, been paid by him for other things. He has very distinctive markings and a particular way of moving. I climbed the bushes as he left. I saw him clearly in the light of the stars and moon. I've always made it my business to know who pays me."

"It could not have been someone else? Perhaps someone who hates Sir Rollo and would wrongfully condemn him?"

"No, I don't believe so."

The counselor looked at his client with regret. The renegade was hauled away. Gabriel thought he saw Rex smile.

The Chief Enforcer spoke to Ganton. "Ganton, come before this assembly and tell what you know about this crime."

Ganton moved to the front, bowed low and rose. He described his position as chief of Sir Rudy's personal guards, his meeting with Rex, their decision to watch from the ruin, the battle, and his capture of the renegade. "While we were binding him, he cursed loudly. I heard him say quite plainly, 'Sir Rollo, you'll die with me--I swear it.' He kept repeating it as my warriors dragged him away," he concluded.

Sir Rollo's counselor again asked permission to question the witness. "Ganton, have you ever heard that there are some who would plot something like this and try to condemn another for it?"

"Yes, I have, but I know what I heard that renegade say. Sir Rollo's jealousy of Sir Rudy is well known. I heard Sir Rollo threaten him many times when I sat with Sir Rudy for his protection in the Board Chamber."

Gabriel saw Rex smile again when Ganton was thanked for his testimony and excused. It went much the same with Rufus. Gabriel was called next.

"What can you add to this?" the Chief Enforcer asked him.

"I have nothing to add that is any different, Lord Chief Enforcer. I saw and heard things pretty much as Rufus said," Gabriel replied. He had never been much good at lies and felt very uncomfortable with the whole situation. His face must have shown it, because Sir Rollo's counselor pounded him with questions. How had he felt? What had he seen? Where had he been standing? He asked the same things over and over. It confused Gabriel, and in his nervousness he began to contradict himself.

"You see what I mean, Lord Chief Enforcer? This creature has been told by someone exactly what he should say," the counselor shouted. "Now he can't get it straight because all of it is a lie!"

Gabriel's pods began to shake and his antennae twitched. He knew what would happen if he didn't pull himself together. Suddenly he realized it was exactly the same feeling he had had during the attack. "Stop it! Stop it!" he screamed. "You are the one confusing me. You make me feel like I did that day, afraid for my life, and I have nothing to be blamed for. I was frightened and confused that day, and you make me live through it again. I told you, it was like Rufus said!"

His outburst made quite an impression on the Chief Enforcer, for he turned on Sir Rollo's counselor. "That's enough of this nonsense. You have had two time frames to try to prove this ridiculous theory that your client was wrongfully accused. It hasn't worked, so you take to harassing these witnesses. Gabriel, thank you for your statement. You are excused."

Gabriel bowed humbly and returned to his place, every part of his body quaking.

The Chief Enforcer spoke again. "Counselor, have you any others to speak in behalf of your client? If so, call them quickly."

"Yes, I do. Sir Rollo's mate, Rachel, will testify that he was at home all evening when the renegade claims to have spoken to him. Now, we will hear someone speak the truth, instead of what they were instructed to say. This will prove what I have been saying all along."

"Rachel, legal mate of Rollo, come forward," the Chief Enforcer stated.

From the very back of the chamber, came a middle-aged female roach. She must have been extremely beautiful in her youth, but the season cycles had not been kind to her. Still, she moved to the front with dignity and grace.

"Where was Sir Rollo at the time in question?" the Chief Enforcer asked her.

She looked at her mate with a coldness Gabriel had never seen. He tried to imagine what she might be feeling at that moment, but he could not. Then she looked toward Rex with eyes that pleaded for mercy and said, "I cannot say for certain whether or not Rollo was at Bush Row that night, but he wasn't with me. I know he went to the shanties to be with his favorite female. He was very agitated when he came home around midnight. He did not speak to me, but paced nervously and then left again, and did not return until dawn. The next day I heard that the female he went to see was found dead. And that, all of you, is the truth."

Every creature in the chamber was so surprised by her words that for several moments it was completely silent. Never before in any Formal Inquiry had a female spoken against her legal mate. Sir Rollo's and his counselor's mandibles opened in shock. Her words made fools of both of them.

Rollo's counselor was the first to find his voice. "Rachel, why are you saying this? We discussed this last evening."

"Oh, shut up," she said. "You said you wanted the truth and you got it. This whole thing is a farce. I could have stood here and lied and said he was with me, and he would still have been condemned. I don't know if he is guilty of this plot or not, but there are plenty of other things he is guilty of that I do know about. Rollo, you were never faithful to me. Why should I protect you? I hope the mantis enjoys its meal."

She turned to the Chief Enforcer. "Lord Chief Enforcer, now you can condemn him without wondering. I beg for your mercy, and make this humble request. When you decide the credit judgment, remember my words. Let me have some dignity for what remains of my life. I have one son left to support through training. He and I are not guilty of anything." She flattened herself into the most humble position possible.

The Chief Enforcer spoke. "Rachel, this Formal Inquiry thanks you for your statement. You are excused."

Rachel rose slightly and returned to her place.

"Rollo," the Chief Enforcer continued, "there now seems to be no doubt that you are guilty of conspiracy to commit murder. I declare before all here that you will be taken to the Center for the Condemned. Your mandibles will be removed tomorrow and you will be delivered to the mantis compound at dawn the next day. All your assets are hereby confiscated. After the costs associated with this case have been paid, the rest, including ownership of your plastic mine, will be granted to Sir Rudy's son as restitution for the death of his father, according to the law. However, because of the unusual situation this day, I will make one other provision. Rachel may retain possession of the domicile in which she lives, and will receive a living allowance each time frame from the profits of his mine, until such time as her last son has gainful employment. Then the son can support his mother. Son of Sir Rudy, is that agreeable with you?"

Rex's thoughts had been racing all this time, as he realized that Sir Rollo must have arrived very shortly after he had killed the female in her shanty home. He was glad he had planned so carefully. Rachel's words were an extra bit of luck. "Yes, Lord Chief Enforcer, I agree. My father is now avenged. I can sleep in peace and begin my life again. This day eases my grief." Even as he spoke the words, he vowed inwardly that if females now felt they could speak against their mates and receive compensation, he would never take a legal mate. He preferred paid females anyway, no responsibilities.

Sir Rollo's ornament, which he had been allowed to wear throughout his confinement and the inquiry, was taken from him and given to Rex. Rex now had seven votes on The Board: his own legitimate vote, granted just before they began the negotiations with the ants, five he inherited from his father, and this one. Each ornament was cast in shining metal and engraved with the same symbol as the Banner of Roacheria. At twenty-four season cycles, he was the youngest ever to wear that many ornaments. He planned to get many more.

    *   *   *   *

Rex sat in the victim's gallery in the Center for the Condemned the next day and watched as the renegade and Rollo had their mandibles cut off. He also watched the following day as they were pushed through the iron gate of the mantis compound.

Rex admired the design of the mantis compound. Its thirty f-unit stone walls slanted slightly inward to prevent condemned roaches or the captive mantises from escaping. The compound was open to the sky--since mantises and many other insects had lost their wings in the evolutionary process. Within the walls, which enclosed an area about two-hundred by three-hundred f-units, the mantises enjoyed a natural setting of meadow grass, small wood plants and a pond. His father had taken him there once right after his final molt into adulthood. They had watched as a common bandit had hidden for an h-unit and then tried to outrun a mantis. Rex was a little disappointed that Rollo and the renegade did not attempt to run or hide. They simply sat down and awaited their fate.

14.

*A*deline sat in Alyssa's work chamber waiting for her to arrive. It was very early in the morning, long before the start of the usual work day. Beside herself with anxiety, she gave up trying to control her emotions and cried. She felt a gentle touch on the back of her thorax.

Alyssa's voice was soft. "Let it out, Adeline." Alyssa handed her a soft cloth and stroked her. "Have some floral herb tea."

Adeline sipped the tea and regained her composure. "I'm sorry. Forgive me for making you come here so early. I should have waited until your work day began."

"Don't be sorry. What's troubling you?"

"Something must be very wrong. I know Henry would write to me. Yet, there is nothing. The others have not written either. I feel in every fiber of my being that something terrible has happened. For the last several days I have meditated each evening. Last night I had a dream that was so real I awoke screaming and could not go back to sleep. It took my sister nearly an h-unit to calm me down. In my dream, I saw Henry,

Herbert, and Howard meditating together. It was a horrible place where they were. I can't even begin to describe it. Howard was on a cushion and he was injured. I heard no voices, but I could feel them calling out for help. I thought perhaps it was my own unfounded fears that produced the dream. But I was so troubled I went to see Herbert's father, even though it was the middle of the night. He told me he had a similar dream two days ago, and said I should come to you at once. There must be some way to contact them. I can't wait a third time frame until the traders come again."

"Have you spoken to Howard's daughter?"

"No, I felt I'd gotten enough creatures up at a bad hour."

"She came by yesterday. She had the same dream, too. I'm going to call an emergency session of our council and recommend that we send a special envoy to Roacheria. I'll compose the communication myself. If the council agrees, we'll have the envoy wait for an answer. I will also recommend a fire ant guard escort. We must have some reassurance that the agreement is being honored by them."

"I'm sorry to cause so much trouble."

"No, don't be sorry. It's right that you came to me. I would be unfit to lead this colony if I didn't act. I asked them to go. I'm responsible for their welfare. I will send word to you as soon as the council decides, and I'll let you know Roacheria's answer the moment it arrives." She held Adeline close and stroked her. "Will you be all right? Shall I send someone home with you?"

"No, thank you, I think I'll be all right."

Adeline returned home. Her sister urged her to go on to work. "I know it may sound hard, but the best way to handle this is to keep busy. Your normal routine will make the time go faster until you hear from Alyssa. The nursery supervisor will understand if you tell her about it." She tried to reassure her sister. "I'm sure they're all right."

*   *   *   *

Rex stood at the rim of the mine pit, watching the workers below as they sat for their noon meal. He noticed that Gabriel was sitting next to Henry and the two were drawing, even as they ate. They nodded to each other and occasionally one of them called to Rufus, who was seated close by. Rufus came to him daily and reported their progress, so he knew that Howard was being carried to the work site, and that the work was progressing quickly. He left the rim and went toward the ants' quarters for the first time since the day he had inspected the portal.

The entrance guards bowed respectfully as he went in. He shook his head in disbelief at the painted images and the coverlets. He looked carefully at the wood heater and the vent system Gabriel had constructed. In spite of his personal feelings, he had to admire Gabriel's technical abilities.

He looked at the parchments on the work surfaces. He could guess which was Henry's. It had an image of a female ant on top of everything else. He wondered why his father had insisted on having this one who was so obviously attached to a female, and then looked through more of the parchments on Henry's work surface. As he saw more and more of the detailed designs, the perfection of the curves in the drawings, the complexity of the equations and calculations, he realized why. This was sheer talent--genius perhaps. This ant had knowledge far beyond anything he would ever understand. He sighed in envy and returned to his work chamber.

His female attendant greeted him when he returned. "Sir, someone named Rachel is waiting for you within. She has a nearly grown male nymph with her."

He nodded and entered. The moment he did so, Rachel prostrated herself before him and hissed to her son, "Get down now, the way I showed you."

Rex acknowledged their humility by tipping his antennae. "Why have you come?"

"Son of Sir Rudy, I wished to thank you in person for your mercy toward me and my son and to swear loyalty to you," Rachel whispered.

He nodded and looked at the male nymph. The youth looked to be about a season cycle away from his final molt into adulthood, a good age to mold into a faithful worker.

The nymph said, "Son of Sir Rudy, I owe my existence and my chance at a decent life to you. I will always be indebted to you and will serve you all my adult life to the best of my ability."

"I believe you will. Go outside now and wait for your mother."

He obediently rose half way and backed out of the chamber, never raising his eyes or antennae.

Rex looked at Rachel. "You deserve the same respect I once gave my own mother. Tell me, why did you speak against your mate?"

"I detested him even more than you did, and he would have been condemned no matter what I said. I have to keep on living, Son of Sir Rudy. I did it hoping that I would be here today to say I will serve you in whatever manner you may ask."

Rex looked at her and recalled something his father had told him when he first went to work. *"Get rid of your enemies, but keep their families loyal to you."*

"Go home, Rachel. Raise that son of yours. Send him here to reaffirm his loyalty to me twice a season cycle. When he finishes his basic training, I may find a way to make use of him. As for you, be sure you let it be known how merciful I am to those who are loyal to me. If I ever have any other use for you, I'll send word."

"You have my eternal gratitude," she said, backing slowly out of the chamber.

Rex had another visitor later that same day, a Board Member about ten season cycles older than his father. Sir Rodger had not come to visit right after Sir Rudy was killed, but Rex knew it was because his mate was ill. She had died since then. Rex considered Sir Rodger basically harmless, perhaps a little crazy because of his unconventional ideas when it came to dealing with The Combined Colonies. He had considerable wealth, but not much influence. Sir Rodger stayed out of the political squabbles between Board Members, and no one had ever managed to accuse him of anything successfully. In Roacheria it was an oddity for a Board Member not to have done something on the shady side of "legal" at some point in life. Sir Rodger was such an oddity.

Out of respect for his age, Rex stooped slightly and swept his pods out to the sides. Sir Rodger nodded in acknowledgment and returned the gesture. "I'm sorry it has taken me so long to come and pay my respects, Son of Sir Rudy."

"I quite understand. I was sorry to hear about your mate," Rex replied.

"One can't live forever. At least she saw our youngest daughter properly mated. You may know him. His name is Reginald."

"Yes, I think we met once during training. Pity you had only daughters. What will you do with your Board Vote when you retire?" he asked, eyeing Sir Rodger's ornament.

Sir Rodger laughed. "Nice try. My vote is not for sale. I'm preparing Reginald to take it over, teaching him everything I know."

There was an awkward silence. Rex finally broke it. "Would you care for some refreshments, Sir Rodger?"

"No, thank you. I won't take much of your time. I really came to congratulate you and offer a bit of advice, which you probably don't want, but I'll give it anyway."

"What do you mean by congratulations?"

"Oh, come, come, Rex. There is no need for us to play games within these four walls. I was referring to your victory in the Formal Inquiry. Rollo didn't do it. I know it because he was with me that night, all upset over finding that his favorite shanty female had killed herself."

"Why didn't you speak up for him?"

Sir Rodger laughed softly. "I didn't hatch yesterday. I haven't lived this long by speaking up for lost causes. No, no, someone went to a great deal of careful planning to pin it on him. He would have been condemned no matter what I or anyone else might have said. No one had any proof that someone else planned it. Of course, The Enforcers never looked at the obvious, at the one who had the most to gain from getting rid of both your father and Rollo. You know, I used to think that if there were a prize in Roacheria for the most ruthless roach, Rollo and your father would have had to share it. Now it appears we have a new champion. That's a little joke I'll undoubtedly take to my own covering place."

"What are you implying with such an insult?"

"Nothing. Now, the piece of advice I promised. Be careful what path you choose in this world, young Sir Rex. Sooner or later, in one way or another, everything we do comes back to us. Be nice to your ant employees. The last thing you need is several legions of fire ants breathing down your thorax to rescue them. Every time you think you can get the best of them, remind yourself how much you enjoy that imported grasshopper. We and the ants need each other, and we should respect that."

Rex twitched an antennae but said nothing, concluding that Sir Rodger was insane. He would bide his time patiently. The day would come when Sir Rodger would make a small mistake and he would be there to take advantage of it, and besides, no one lived forever.

"Well, I thank you for your time. I know how busy you are,"Sir Rodger said, rising to leave. As he reached the portal he said, "By the way, if you ever really want to know who killed your father, go to a quiet pond and look into the water." With that, he left.

*   *   *   *

The following sixthday, as he relaxed at home, Rex was interrupted by one of his female servants. "Excuse me, Sir, but someone from The Board is here and he says it's urgent."

Rex sighed and went to the parlor where he found The Supreme Executor of the Board waiting for him. He bowed respectfully. "To what do I owe this unexpected pleasure, Sir?"

"Son of Sir Rudy, I know we said you could do business as you pleased concerning these ant engineers, but what exactly are you doing?"

"They are training my tunneler in their methods, Sir."

"You may have a problem. There is a legion of fifty fire ants camped a quarter d-unit from the west sentry post. They arrived carrying a grassfrond and a message. It's an official communication addressed to your father and The Board. They are waiting for an answer. Apparently, they are under the impression that their agreement is with The Board. I don't need any incidents that will provoke the wrath of the Combined Colonies. You can do anything you like except start a war. I'm very fond of imported grasshopper and we all enjoy the profits from plastic trade. Here is the communication they sent, something about not sending letters. Our communications workers only translated the first few lines and said that the best interpreter is already working for you."

"Thank you, Sir. I had anticipated something of this nature. I can handle this. You needn't worry about anything."

"Good. I'll see you at our next regular meeting," said the Supreme Executor as he turned to leave.

Rex called his head servant. "Send for Rufus and bring him to my work chamber as soon as he arrives." He left the parlor to think about his response.

Rufus arrived an h-unit later and bowed low. "You sent for me, Sir?"

"Yes, I've been informed that a group of fire ants are camped on our surface area waiting for a response to this," he said, handing the parchment to Rufus. "So tell me what they want."

Rufus read:

> "To The South East Roach Control Board and Sir Rudy,
>
> When we negotiated the contract with you, we were told that we could send and would receive letters on a regular basis. Over two time frames have passed and we have not received anything, not even any official communications. We are very concerned and have sent this special envoy to pick up any letters written by Henry, Herbert, and Howard. Their families are anxious to hear from them and are concerned about their welfare. We peacefully await your reply."

"It's signed, 'Alyssa, Council Chief, South Harvester Colony 45'," Rufus concluded.

Rex had before him his copy of the agreement. "There is nothing in the agreement about letters. How did that subject come up in your discussions?"

"Henry's Promised One asked about it. Your father had me tell her that they could write, but that visits wouldn't be possible. I made up something about visits being dangerous because of bandits on the trail. The first time frame, when you kept the letters, I told them that bandits had attacked and destroyed their letters."

Rex began to laugh. "Oh, you are good, Rufus! You have given me the perfect response. Wait a moment while I write this, then you translate it and take it to them. I promise you a large bonus if you smooth this over. Take about fifty of my personal warriors with you when you go. I'll give you more instructions in a moment, and I'll give the warriors their orders."

*   *   *   *

Adeline entered Alyssa's work chamber. A few moments later, Howard's daughter and Herbert's father arrived.

Alyssa greeted all of them. "Thank you for coming. Commander Ferdinand returned safely not long ago. He's on his way here." She poured tea for all of them. The fire ant commander arrived before they finished it.

After greetings and introductions, he began to relate the events of his journey into Roacheria. "I wish I had better news, but at least we know what's going on. I'd forgotten how bleak the surface can seem at this time of the season cycle, or maybe it's just the trail through the ruins, but I had the strangest feeling the whole trip. We never saw a single living creature, yet I felt I was being watched. We held the grassfrond before us at all times, so that anyone could see our peaceful intentions.

"We sat by one of their outposts for quite a while before anyone approached. I held out the grassfrond and tried to signal them to come toward us. One finally did, and I held out your letter to the South East Roach Control Board. He spoke no Ant, but I finally made him understand that he should take the letter and we would wait for an interpreter."

"Did they take you to where Henry and the others are?" Adeline interrupted.

"No, they didn't, but I understand why. We made ourselves as comfortable as we could, and ate and drank from the supplies we carried. Nearly three h-units later, about fifty warriors arrived. We jumped to our pods, but their interpreter shouted in Ant not to be alarmed. It turned out to be Rufus. The warriors circled us completely, but faced outward, so they could see in every direction. Rufus introduced himself to me. He apologized for alarming us and said that Sir Rudy's son had sent the warriors for our protection. He asked if we had been attacked on our journey. When I said we had not, his response was, 'That's fortunate. They must have been sleeping off last night's ale.' I tell you, I'll never understand roaches."

He twitched his antennae, shifted on his cushion, and continued. "Rufus went on to tell us that some renegades, fearful that having ants come to work in their plastic mines would mean that Roacherian workers would have their jobs taken away, attacked Sir Rudy and our members the day they went to Roacheria. Sir Rudy's warriors arrived in time to rescue Herbert, Henry, Howard, Rufus, and Gabriel, but Sir Rudy was brutally murdered. Their authorities caught some of them and condemned them, but many escaped. The Board thought it would be easy to catch the others, so they did not inform us. Since then, these renegades have stirred up many and caused a lot of trouble. The traders were attacked the end of the first time frame. The letters were stolen and destroyed in anger. They were afraid to send letters with the next group."

Alyssa spoke up. "Remember how dangerous Rufus said the ruins area could be?"

The others nodded. Commander Ferdinand went on with his report. "Rufus said that The Board has decided that for everyone's safety, they will only send traders every other time frame. They will send them with many warriors, and say that we should have our guards meet them at the bridge. They will send formal communications at those times. They will inform us when they have these renegades under control. I told Rufus that if they would provide for the needs of all their citizens, as we do, they probably wouldn't have such violent crime. Like I said earlier, I'll never understand them."

Commander Ferdinand paused to sip his tea. "Henry, Herbert and Howard are safe. They were taken to a secure setting close to the mine, where they are guarded day and night for their protection. Rufus said renegades have approached the mine twice but were driven off by the warriors. He apologized that their living quarters were not as pleasant as the ones Sir Rudy's son had originally prepared, but that this was necessary. He also said he was glad that letters had only been discussed orally and not guaranteed. Under the present circumstances, it would be impossible for them to guarantee that any communications we sent would arrive."

Adeline's head drooped. "We are to hear nothing then? And they are still in danger?"

"I'm afraid that's correct. But at least we know they are safe, and we understand what's happened."

Alyssa shook her head. "I wish we hadn't acted in haste. Everything seemed so good."

Commander Ferdinand set down his mug. "It was late in the day by then, so we prepared to camp for the night. Sir Rudy's son sent us fuel and fresh provisions. The warriors guarded us through the night, so we slept well. They stayed with us the next morning as we returned. One time, we saw some renegades in the distance. Some of the warriors ran toward them screaming that terrifying battle cry of theirs. They fled."

"Rufus mentioned that when he was here, too; that bandits ran from Sir Rudy's warriors,"Alyssa recalled.

"Rufus also told us that the work on the mine tunnel is going very slowly. Apparently the tunnel was in much worse shape than the roaches thought. Our engineers had to pull a controlled collapse and start it all over again. Howard was injured when a support timber gave in before they were ready.

"Don't worry," he said to Howard's daughter. "Sir Rudy's son sent his own physician to treat it. It was a simple appendage fracture. He'll be fine. However, Rufus said it may take longer than the originally agreed upon six time frames to complete the work. They want to know if we will live up to our part of the agreement and see that it is completed. We're to send an answer with our credit payment for plastic in two time frames when the traders come under this new schedule.

"Here is Rufus' translation of the formal communication from Sir Rudy's son. It states most of what I've told you," he concluded, handing Alyssa the parchment.

It was silent in the chamber for several minutes. Adeline sighed. Writing in her journal would never fill the aching loneliness she felt inside. Knowing that it might be longer than four more time frames, and not knowing how much longer it would be, seemed too much at the moment. She clenched her mandibles together for control. Although no one would blame her for letting her feelings out, she preferred to do that in private.

"Of course we must be true to ourselves and keep our part of the agreement," Alyssa finally said. "I wish that we had not begun it, but our honor is at stake. I'll send the communication when the time comes. I signed that agreement and I must fulfill my duty, too. I know Howard, and Henry, and Herbert feel the same about their work. None of us could do otherwise. I will also announce in the Colonial Bulletin that everyone in this colony should support them with our daily meditations."

She reached out to Adeline, Herbert's father, and Howard's daughter. "This is a time for us to join our minds and hearts more closely, support each other's needs, and show even greater care for each other."

They linked their front pods and raised them in meditation for several minutes. The simple touch of other pods strengthened Adeline. She offered no words in thought, but absorbed the strength of the others.

15.

*H*enry was pleased with Gabriel's progress in learning their methods. More than once he had written in his journal that Gabriel was the only good thing about the whole project. Howard frequently complimented his ability to teach. One evening, Henry offered Gabriel some of their food. It was quite late and he knew the roach must be as hungry as he was. Gabriel shook his head but gestured that Henry should go ahead and eat. Henry handed him another diagram to complete and began his evening meal.

Voices came from outside the portal. Rufus entered. The three ants looked at him, hoping the long awaited letters had finally arrived. Rufus lowered his head and let his antennae droop.

"What's the matter?" Herbert asked.

Rufus looked down. "I've just come from a meeting with Sir Rudy's son. I had to wait a long time, since he had been delayed in a Board Meeting. The Board will not allow any more attempts at sending and receiving letters. Sir Rudy's son argued that there had been a verbal understanding about letters, but the other members said, 'No.' They said it's too expensive to send so many warriors to insure that bandits do not attack. We hoped that after the renegade was condemned, the raids would stop, but the renegade leader had many friends, if you can call them that, and they are causing a lot of trouble. The Board decided that they will only send traders every other time frame. They will take twice the amount of plastic, but will only carry official messages from The Board to your Colony Council. Sir Rudy's son was very disappointed, and now I have had to pass this unfortunate news to you."

Howard lifted his head from his sleep cushion. Although he directed the work each day from the cushioned basket, he needed extra rest in the evenings. "What do you mean? We saw that all those who attacked us were killed, except the leader. We watched your warriors take him away. How can there be more?"

"The leader didn't bring all of his band with him that day. The others are angry that he was captured. They are the ones causing problems now."

Henry stared at Rufus. "Why can't they take at least one letter from each of us with the official communications?"

Rufus shook his antennae. "The Board refuses to allow it. They said that it was not specifically mentioned in the contract you signed. I know it's not fair to you, but that's how it's going to be. I can't do anything about it. Gabriel may only stay an h-unit after the regular work day from now on. Sir Rudy's son wants the two of us safely escorted away from the mine before dark each evening. We'll see you tomorrow."

After the portal had closed behind the two roaches, and Henry heard the familiar sound of the timber sliding into place to prevent their exit, he picked up the stack of letters he had ready to send, methodically crumpled them, and threw them across the chamber. "I should have refused. I could have, you know. I should have stayed home and let Dennis come! Everyone would have understood. I never wanted this!" He paced about in anger, picked up the crumpled papers and tore them to shreds. Then he pounded out his frustration on the portal. When his pods ached from pounding, he slumped to the floor in silence.

"It's all right, Henry," Howard said. "Let your anger out. Would you like more parchment to tear up?"

Herbert sat down beside him and handed him some water. "I'd give you tea, but we're all out." He stroked Henry to calm him.

Henry finished the water. "I'm sorry. I've made a fool of myself." He began to clean up the mess he had made.

"Don't be," said Howard. "It's always better to let it out than to let the anger eat you up inside. I'm glad you chose to come. I know Dennis. He's a good engineer, but he doesn't know how to teach. He'll never make a good mentor. Come closer. Let's meditate together. We must take care of each other; we are all we have."

*   *   *   *

Rufus and Gabriel walked away from the mine--no escort anywhere. "I'm beginning to understand a lot of what you say to them. Tell me something, how do you manage to keep track of it all?" Gabriel asked.

"Keep track of what?"

"The lies you tell them. One of these days you're going to contradict yourself and the whole thing will fall apart."

"No, I won't." Rufus replied. "I'm always consistent."

Gabriel shook his antennae. "You owe your life to ants. Doesn't it ever bother you, what you are doing to them?"

Rufus was silent a moment. He stopped and looked right at Gabriel. "Leave me alone about it, will you? I don't need you for a conscience. You want to know how I do it? I refuse to think about it, that's how. I think about how much credit I'm getting. Do you know that I've paid off everything I owe? Besides that, I'll have all I need for my nymph to get really good training when he's grown. I don't want him to have to live like I do. I'm only doing my job. Forget it and do yours, too. At least I don't get stepped on."

Gabriel glared at him. "There's more than one way to be stepped on, Rufus. Have you no pride at all?"

Rufus glared back. "We all do what we have to do. Don't keep reminding me. My job is hard enough. Half of me wishes I'd never heard of Sir Rudy. It was always so easy before. I went into a colony, completed the deal, and left. I never had to see them afterward, and I never went back to the same colony twice. Now, I have to break it to these three easily, keep South Harvester 45 happy, and satisfy all of Sir Rex's demands. Don't get me started. You don't really want to know what I know. Learn to dig your tunnels and stay out of my business." He scurried away into the night, leaving Gabriel alone.

*   *   *   *

About half way through the fourth time frame, as Gabriel sat with the ants at lunch, he worked up his courage to ask them something through Rufus. Rufus explained. "Henry, Gabriel doesn't want to be disrespectful, and he doesn't want to offend you, but he wants to ask you about colony life. Is that all right?"

"What does he want to know?"

"He said that while he was on the colony tour he saw your Council Chief, Alyssa, stop to help a refuse gatherer. Something like that would never happen here. Refuse gatherers are the lowest of the low. He doesn't understand why she did that."

Henry spoke slowly and stopped every sentence or two, so that Rufus could translate. "To start, I don't understand 'lowest of the low'. You see, with us, nobody is 'above' anybody else. We all know we need each other, and that every job in a colony is essential. The refuse gatherer is just as important as the Council Chief. Where would the Council be without someone to clean the colony? Where would the refuse gatherer be without the Council to take care of managing things? One is no more, or no less, important than the other. We choose our life's work according to naturally given skills and our interests. All of us try many things during training. That way, we appreciate others who do work that we find too hard for us or what you might call demeaning."

Henry paused to eat some seeds. "My Promised One, Adeline, works in a larva nursery. She is very happy. I spent a time frame in one. Although I cherish larvae and look forward to caring for ours after we mate, I don't have the patience to care for a whole chamber full of them. I also spent time with my father in the reuse center. It was good work, but I could not use my skills in drawing and problem solving there. I explored at least twenty-five different jobs before I finally chose tunnel engineering."

Henry stopped again. "Hand me that water flask, please." Thirst satisfied, he continued. "We respect and appreciate everyone. Think about it. Could you or the mine workers get by without each other? Could Sir Rudy's son get his plastic without any of you?"

"How do you determine the amount of credit for a job?" Gabriel asked next. "Doesn't the Council Chief get more?"

"It's not the job, but the needs of the individuals," Henry explained. "Someone who is young and not mated requires very little.

When there are larvae in a family, they need more credit for the plastic. Some families have many larvae, some only one. With no way to know the number of eggs a female will lay, why should some larvae suffer because they happen to hatch into a large family? We all work and take only what is needed. We reaffirm our way of life every Last Day. What would we do with more?"

"We buy more expensive things and more of them," Rufus stated.

"What's the point of that? What do you do with all you accumulate?"

Rufus had no answer.

Gabriel chewed the last of his lunch. Finally he said, "What a wonderful system you have. I wish it could be that way here."

Rufus translated his statement to Henry, and then said to Gabriel in Roach, "Get your head out of the clouds! We have to live in our own reality."

Each day after that, Gabriel would ask something else about colony life. He began to understand a philosophy very different from his own.

One evening in the ants' chamber, Henry heard Rufus snap at Gabriel.

"Rufus, what is it Gabriel wants to know?" Henry asked.

"Nothing you want to answer. He's getting rude and personal."

"Is it about Adeline?"

"Yes, I keep telling him what you told me about personal questions."

"I was angry with you on the trail coming here because you asked after laughing with Sir Rudy. You mocked my pain in leaving her. Gabriel asks me things respectfully, because he wants to learn. There is a difference. I will answer him and not take offense."

Rufus sighed. "He wants to know about your promise and how you will unite formally. I told him there is some sort of ceremony where you vow to cherish each other, but I never went to one. He wants to know what 'cherish' means. It's not a word that translates well."

Henry set down the parchment he had been preparing. "On the day we give ourselves to each other, each of our families will carry us in baskets to the portal of a meditation chamber. We will get out of our baskets, take each other's pods, and lead our families and friends in. When everyone is seated, we will stand before them and begin the ceremony. I will speak first. I will give Adeline a gift that symbolizes what she means to me. I think it will be a rock, because she has stood by solidly and waited so long for me. Then she will speak and give me her symbolic gift."

He picked up the ink pot. "We will join our front pods and rise like this," he said, drawing a picture of a male and female ant, nearly upright, front pods linked high above their heads. "We will say the words we spoke when we made our promise, 'I promise myself to you as your mate, to cherish and support, no matter what joys or sorrows may occur. I will nurture with joy all new life that may come from our union. I promise this freely as long as we both live in this world.'"

Both roaches looked at Henry with sincere interest.

"After that, we, and all those gathered to share our joy, will break and eat seeds, like we do on Last Day, and at other times when we wish to show our care for each other. Adeline and I will speak to all gathered, offering our work to our colony, as we have offered ourselves to each other. Those gathered will accept our gifts and promise their support to us in any way we need it. We will write our names and the date into the *Record of the Mated* for our colony."

Henry stopped a minute so Rufus could finish translating. He watched as Gabriel smiled, and then he continued. "After the ceremony is over, we will lead all our friends into a banquet chamber and we will celebrate. We will eat foods that everyone brought to share, and have our mating cake--a large, oval honey cake. It's shape symbolizes an egg, because we hope to create new life. Larvae should hatch into a family where a male and female are committed to each other."

Gabriel gave him a confused look.

Rufus said, "I'm not sure what you mean either."

Henry explained further. "You see, larvae have no pods. They cannot give to others. They must receive all the feelings the male and female have for each other. They must be wanted, cuddled, nurtured with physical and emotional food for whole health. After about seven season cycles, when a larva is full of everything we can give to it, it curls in on itself and goes to sleep, as if to ponder all it has received. We nourish it with needed plastic and let it sleep in pupation. When it emerges as an adult, it has pods to reach out and give to others what it received, and a mind to understand and learn about life."

"Aah," Gabriel said when Rufus had finished translating.

Henry continued. "After the mating cake is eaten by all, we will begin our mating dance. The music will start out slowly. Adeline and I will stand on opposite sides of the chamber and move like this." He demonstrated the back and forth steps and began a small spiral. He also drew two inward spiraling lines on parchment, the shape of the dance when seen from above. "In the most ancient times, before all ants were either male or female, the queen of a new colony would fly into the air in a spiral with the drones following her. Now, we have no more wings, so the dance is done on the ground. The music will go faster and faster as we get closer to each other and finally meet in the middle. Our families and friends will join in the dancing and we will continue to celebrate.

"Finally, we will climb into one basket and our families will carry us together to our new home. We will have a quarter time frame alone to give ourselves to each other completely, for we can give our gift of life but once. All our young, even season cycles later, will be from that one giving. That is why we mate for life. I would do anything to make Adeline happy. She is everything to me. I would even die for her, because I cherish her."

Gabriel looked at the drawing of the dance. "That's the shape of your tunnel."

"Yes," Henry said when Rufus had translated his comment. "I built it that way for her."

Gabriel took Henry's front pods in his, the way Rufus had taught him to do a friendly ant greeting, and said very slowly in Ant, "Thank you, Henry. I understand 'cherish.'"

Henry turned the greeting into an embrace. "You're welcome."

Rufus and Gabriel walked away from the mine in silence that night. Gabriel was thinking about all he had heard. He thought about what he felt for his own mate. He wondered what would happen if he gave her more affection. How would she respond? In the dusk of late evening, he picked a few of the spring blossoms that were blooming along the way. Rufus watched him and shook his head.

*   *   *   *

Work on the tunnel proceeded smoothly. Howard had Gabriel begin to direct more of the work himself. Henry sent partially completed charts home with Gabriel each evening. Gabriel would complete them at home and Henry would check them the next day. Gabriel made fewer and fewer mistakes.

Gabriel kept every parchment he was given, and traced Henry's problem charts so that he had two copies: one unfinished, and one with his work and Henry's corrections. He knew the information would be helpful when he was called upon to train others.

Gabriel also continued to try to learn Ant. It was not a difficult language. He found that he could usually understand what they were saying if they spoke slowly, but he couldn't remember the right words when he tried to speak it.

They finished the tunnel half way through the sixth time frame. Gabriel brought a jug of ale. They filled their mugs right there in the mine, and included the roach tunnel diggers they had trained.

*   *   *   *

"You can go in," the attendant told Rufus.

Rufus entered cautiously, stooping low. Rex stood and smiled. Relieved to see his good mood, Rufus said, "The tunnel is complete, Sir. Your mine can begin regular production tomorrow. Would you like to go down and inspect it?"

"I will later. Tell the ants that for the next two quarter time frames, since their contract is not up, I will be moving them to my new mine, the one I was granted by the Formal Inquiry as restitution for my father's death. Have them inspect all the tunnels thoroughly and begin work on the worst area. No more of those controlled collapses. We do things my way now. When the time frame ends, you know what you are to tell them. I assume you will continue to work for me."

"Of course, Sir. I'll tell them to gather their things tonight. What time would you like them ready?"

"I'll send a column of warriors to escort them at dawn. Tell Gabriel I want to see him."

*   *   *   *

Ecstatic from their "celebration" and his own accomplishment in learning, Gabriel nearly floated into Sir Rex's work chamber, but he remembered to stoop respectfully. "Here at your request, Sir."

"Sit down," Rex said. "You've learned well. I've been watching. I've seen some of the charts you've drawn. Since you still have half a time frame with your teachers, I'm sending you and them over to the Number 6 Mine for a while. I want you to go back and forth, half a day there, and half a day here to see to it that this tunnel continues properly as production resumes. Later, I will find someone for you to train. Your contract with me calls for additional compensation for these extra duties. I will listen to a reasonable request."

Gabriel's light mood vanished. He had been thinking a lot about what he would say when this moment came. He knew Rex hated him, and would deceive him if he thought he could. "Sir, instead of an increase in credit, I have a different request. May I make it?"

"I'm listening."

"The mines will always be dangerous places, and others might envy what I've learned. Instead of more credit, I would like to ask you for a Certificate of Assurance for my mate and family. I would like to know that if I die for any reason, my mate will continue to receive my credit until the youngest nymph has completed training and has a good job. Sir, as long as I live, you will have all my work for the present rate."

Rex looked at him long and hard. Gabriel was smarter than he'd thought. He tapped one front pod on his work surface, pondering the advantages of this arrangement. He needed Gabriel for a few season cycles until others could be trained. Gabriel was properly humbled now, and he wanted him to think everything was fine. There would be time later to plan Gabriel's death.

"That's reasonable. I agree to it," he replied. He reached for official mine letter head parchment and wrote the letter. "Here," he said, handing it to Gabriel. "Take it to the Agency for Document Registration. Then there will never be a question between us, and you'll never have to worry about your family. You see, I can be reasonable when I'm properly approached."

"Thank you, Sir," Gabriel replied, rising to leave. "I will be pleased to train whomever you choose."

*   *   *   *

Rufus walked slowly toward the ant's quarters, thinking about what he would say and how to make himself cheerful. He stood outside their portal a moment before going in, listening to the sounds of laughter. The entry guard gave him an odd look. Rufus sighed. "Open the portal."

"Rufus," Howard said cheerfully, "we were wondering how long you would be. We want you to ask Sir Rudy's son if he will finally meet us. We feel the need to celebrate with him, too. Do your customs of grieving allow celebration now?"

Rufus felt luck was with him again. Whenever he ran out of ideas, they would say something that helped him construct another lie. Rex had specifically told him at one point that he did not want his name or face known to them. He had used Rex's grief as an excuse.

"Technically, custom would allow it. Such things are up to the individual, but I don't think he would. Sir Rudy's son is a very private creature. He keeps to himself. It would be a little like me asking you a personal question. Here, grief ends when the individual ends it. However, he does send you greetings and thanks you for a job well done. He also has a request."

"Oh, what is it?" Howard asked.

"Since the terms of the contract you signed state six full time frames, and that time is not quite over, he wants you to travel tomorrow at dawn to the Number 6 Mine. That mine belonged to the one who plotted his father's death and was given to him by the Formal Inquiry. You are to inspect the tunnels there and begin work on the worst one for the time that remains. You will form long range plans for Gabriel to follow."

"We wouldn't accomplish much in such a short time," Howard said.

Henry and Herbert set down their mugs and moved closer to Howard and Rufus.

"No," Rufus agreed, "but the long range planning will help Gabriel. What if those tunnels are really bad and a collapse happened there? You could prevent further tragedy," Rufus said, playing on the statement he remembered Howard making the day they had recovered the last of the bodies.

"Where is this mine?" Howard asked. "You keep telling us how dangerous it is to travel."

"It's about ten d-units south-east of here--not far from the city. Sir Rudy's son will provide guards for your safety, as he does here. He'll provide an escort on your return journey. Sir Rudy's son has always been concerned about your safety."

Howard looked toward the others. Herbert tipped his antennae as if to say, "Whatever you decide is all right."

Henry looked at Rufus. He thought about the constantly rising expense reports, the lack of letters and official communications, and other things that didn't add up. Something had changed about Rufus during the last time frame. Henry was suspicious, but he felt guilty for feeling that way. He wanted to refuse, to demand that they leave for home the next day, but he felt bound by duty and by his written word. He said nothing.

"We will honor the last half time frame of our contract," Howard said.

Rufus nodded. "Good. I'll have the guards bring in some large baskets. Everything here should be packed in them. I don't know what your quarters there will be like, but surely, these furnishings will do for such a short time. It'll save a lot of added expense if you carry your things yourselves. It takes five roaches to carry what one of you can bear. Guards will take whatever you cannot carry. Howard, remember the restrictions the physician gave when he removed the plaster from your leg. You shouldn't carry anything but your own satchel. Your leg will be weaker for another season cycle and you shouldn't risk refracturing it."

"We'll be ready," Howard said.

16.

*H*erbert and Henry carried the most heavily loaded baskets the next morning. Henry thought about all the loads he had carried as he built his tunnel, and he thought about Adeline. A vague sense of foreboding that he could not put into words nagged at his mind. He remembered the trip into Roacheria, how little attention he had paid to his surroundings, and how utterly unprepared he had been for the attack. This time, he paid attention to every wood plant and bush.

There was little conversation as they progressed. Henry noticed that Rufus, in particular, seemed far away from them. He avoided looking at them, and his voice sounded distant when he spoke.

They were not on any sort of trail. Rufus said that it was safer that way. Ganton led the group and the ants were surrounded by thirty warriors. The heat and humidity seemed oppressive for early morning, especially since summer solstice was still a time frame away. Henry shifted the heavy basket into a better position, and hoped they would stop for a rest and some water.

Ahead, he could see oddly shaped heaps of wood and stone, topped with sheets of metal. Pipes protruded from the flat tops, with smoke rising from some of them. Curiosity got the better of Henry.

"Rufus, what are those things ahead of us?" he asked.

"They are the dwellings of some of the workers at the Number 6 Mine. We're nearly there."

"Creatures live in those?"

Rufus hesitated. "Uh . . . Yes, the mine's previous owner let his workers live close to the mine for convenience. Sir Rudy's son let them continue when he took over."

Howard broke in. "You don't mean that we . . ."

"Oh, no, you wouldn't be safe. I wouldn't live there myself. Who can say what is in their minds? But if they didn't like it, I'm sure they wouldn't stay."

A few minutes later, they reached the rim of the pit, which was much wider and deeper than the Number 1 Mine. The slopes were dotted with tunnel entrances in a way that reminded Henry of the image of a honey comb he had seen in one of his basic training manuscripts.

Ganton led them to the east side of the pit toward a small Duo Pod ruin. Its crumbled synthetic stone walls had been reinforced on the outside with dirt. A large, flat, heavy looking sheet of metal formed a slightly slanted roof, and a new, thick wooden portal had been fitted into one side.

"Carry the baskets inside this for now," Rufus instructed them. "We'll rest a few minutes before we begin," he added, passing them large mugs of water.

Howard stared at him. "This place is even worse looking than the other! There must be a hundred tunnels. It'll take several time frames to inspect them all. What can we possibly accomplish in fourteen days?"

Rufus laughed nervously. "They aren't all in use. The upper levels are mined out. There's no more plastic there. The productive areas are at the bottom. The tunnels here are shorter. We will probably inspect several before today is over. Are you ready to begin?"

Uncertainly, the three ants followed Gabriel and Rufus along the path into the pit. It curved back and forth, zig-zagging its way to the bottom. Several roach workers passed them headed up, carrying loads of raw plastic. Henry noticed one who plodded along more slowly than the others. He looked up at Henry, his eyes dull, his expression vacant.

When they came to the first tunnel entrance, Gabriel explained, stopping often for Rufus to translate. "This mine is more typical than the Number 1 Mine. They began with a pit, then tunneled in a short way until the plastic ran out. When they had a ring of short tunnels, like you see around the top, they dug deeper into the pit, found a new layer, mined it out and began with the short tunnels again. This mine has gone down five levels. They have gone three quarters of the way around with the tunnels. When the ring is complete, they will deepen the pit once more and hope they hit a sixth layer of plastic rich soil."

Howard said, "That is a lot like what we do, except there's no pit, and we refill the mined-out tunnels. Do you expect a sixth layer here?"

"Yes, some mines have even more. Sometimes owners dig the pit until they find the bottom limit before beginning any tunnels. The Number 1 Mine has longer tunnels because there are many Duo Pod ruins over it. A wide area of flat synthetic stone near the surface made it hard to dig a pit. But that mine has much more plastic."

They entered the first producing tunnel, walking to the sides, so they didn't interfere with the workers. Gabriel commented to Rufus in Roach, "Old Rollo certainly wasn't stingy with support timbers like someone else we know."

"What did he say?" asked Howard.

Rufus paused before translating. "He said there seem to be plenty of support timbers."

"How long are these tunnels actually in use?" Howard asked.

Gabriel spoke with the mine overseer who had joined them as they entered. Rufus related the reply. "The overseer says it takes about a season cycle to mine out one tunnel. They have three producing tunnels right now and room for several more on this level."

Howard looked at the tunnel walls. "If the tunnels are only used for a season cycle, they may not need to be repaired, if all of them have as many support timbers as this one. I would suggest, however, that the entrances of those no longer in production be filled in for safety reasons. The entrances of those we passed near the top of the rim must be eighty season cycles old by what you said."

After a few moments of conversation between the overseer and Gabriel, Rufus said, "The mine overseer thanks you for your suggestion. Some of the oldest ones fell in long ago. He says plugging the entrances will also cut down on illegal scavenging."

The ants found that since the tunnels in this mine were better supported, they were strong enough as they were. "This is what I think you should recommend to Sir Rudy's son," said Howard. "We can start to train one team here to continue the tunnel using our methods. I think it should be the third one we entered, because it is the shortest and will produce the longest. Continue the other two with your old methods. Gabriel can easily direct work on one here and the one at the other mine. As he trains more of your engineers, more tunnels can be done our way. Does this mine have an engineer like Gabriel?"

"Yes," replied Rufus.

"He should work with us as long as we're here and with Gabriel when we leave."

"I'll take your recommendation to Sir Rudy's son today. I think now would be a good time for you to return to your new quarters and settle your things. It's long past midday and you haven't stopped to eat. Gabriel should come with me to present this proposal. We will return to you in the morning."

Ganton was standing at the rim of the pit when they reached it. He spoke sharply to Rufus and Gabriel and then pointed toward the trail leading away from the mine, raised his other front pod and flicked the tip. Immediately, six warriors who had been standing several f-units away, surrounded the ants.

"Go with them," Rufus said.

As they walked between the warriors, Henry heard Gabriel speaking to Rufus with a questioning tone. Rufus' answer sounded angry.

The two warriors in front stood on either side of the portal when they reached the place where the ants had left their possessions. One of the warriors opened the portal. Two of those behind began to push Howard roughly.

"Where is your respect?" Henry said. Another guard lowered his head and opened his mandibles in a threatening way. He shouted something Henry did not understand and pointed to Henry and the portal. The other guard continued to push.

"Let it go, Henry," Howard said. "We've got to take our furnishings to our new quarters."

The portal banged shut behind them and the three looked about in dismay as they realized that this was where they were expected to live. The workers had dumped the baskets in the middle of the floor. The chamber was littered with dirt and bits of synthetic stone. Dirt was piled up in one corner, still damp from sky water that had fallen before the roof was put on. The walls were so drab it made their old quarters seem pleasant.

Howard was the first to speak. "This is intolerable. We must complain to Rufus as soon as he gets here tomorrow."

Herbert tried to rationalize. "Maybe these warriors don't understand about us. Perhaps this was a premature decision since we finished the other work early, and there wasn't time to prepare. They've left tools and cleaning utinsils here. We might as well use them. I guess I can put up with anything for a short time."

Henry looked at Howard. "I don't like what's happening either, but we can't do anything about it now. Does your satchel still have our lunch in it?"

"Yes," Howard replied.

Henry picked up the broom and cleaned an area large enough for them to sit down to eat. While they were eating, a warrior entered and set down a large container of water. He gave them a hateful look and left quickly.

*   *   *   *

Rex sat quietly as Rufus and Gabriel explained Howard's recommendation to him. "I don't want you to train that tunneler, Gabriel. I spoke with him and he said he never learned the math you say is needed. Plus, he refuses to work with ants. He won't be working for me at all. You go back and forth like I told you. Send five of the ten you've already trained to dig with them in the third tunnel. The other producing tunnels get one fourth less timbers. My cousin is coming from Sea Edge at the start of the next season cycle. I want you to train him. Make a list of the calculation training units you had, so I can search the training centers for others with the necessary background."

"Excuse me, Sir, how will I direct four producing tunnels, two the old way and two the ants' way, when Henry, Herbert, and Howard leave?" Gabriel asked.

Rex twitched his antennae back and forth and said calmly, "They aren't leaving. You're both excused."

After they left Rex, Gabriel asked, "What did he mean, they aren't leaving?"

"Oh, didn't I tell you? The contract has been extended."

Gabriel stared at him. "Don't lie to me! What is going on? Why was Ganton so rude to them and to us?"

"Don't ask questions. Just do your job."

*   *   *   *

"What do you mean, we don't have permission to leave tomorrow?" Henry shouted. "We have completed the contract! The six time frames are up. We don't need anyone's permission to leave. I think we've done more than necessary, putting up with this filthy heat box of a place to live, and being treated so indecently for the last fourteen days."

"Henry, this isn't my fault. I'm trying to explain. If you'll look at these figures and let me finish," Rufus said.

"Henry," Howard said, "we're all hot and tired, and I know the odor is nauseating, but anger won't help right now. Let him finish."

Rufus' pods were unsteady as he laid out Sir Rex's version of their expense reports in order from the first to the sixth time frame. Below each, he laid the ones he had translated. With great attention to detail, he pointed out that the figures were exactly the same. He had not made any errors in translating. Then he carefully added the total of all six.

"You see, the total of all of them is more than the amount you were to be paid. Sir Rudy's son insists that you remain and work for free until the debt to him is paid in full. He was very angry with me yesterday when he added it up. He said his father offered you plenty of credit for the job and you did not use the amount wisely."

"It can't be right," Herbert said. "We added those figures each time frame, ordering less and less so we would remain within the set amount. Why is this last one so much?" He showed his own figures and the changes in the lists from one time frame to the next. "Wait a minute. You have made mistakes. Look, the amounts are different each time for the same items. Here," he pointed, "we received ten weight units of seeds at this cost, and on this one, eight units, and the cost is more than it was for ten!" He went on to note other examples.

Howard now looked at the sixth and final list. "We've been charged for six time frames worth of parchment and other supplies that Sir Rudy said would be provided. It's in the contract."

Rufus looked at their copy of the contract he had written that first evening in South Harvester 45 and recalled Sir Rudy's words, "*Hide the things you need to as we discussed.*"

He pointed to the words. "Parchment and supplies will be provided," and said, "It doesn't say 'free of charge.' Sir Rudy may have intended that but his son is in control now and he goes by the letter of what is stated. In his grief, he has grown bitter. He doesn't say so and he's wrong to think it, but I feel he blames you for his father's death. Believe me, I tried to reason with him. He would hear none of it. I'm afraid you will have to stay and continue to build the tunnel. He has commanded his warriors to see to it that you don't leave until the debt is worked off."

The three ants stared at him, their faces totally blank.

"He would keep us here like slaves?" Henry finally said. "I can't believe I'm hearing this."

Rufus lowered his antennae. "Yes, he will."

Henry's voice expressed fury. "Why didn't you tell us about the other costs sooner? We could have had our colony send us parchment and ink."

Rufus shrunk a little lower. "Do you honestly think that I, who spent a season cycle in one of your colonies being cared for so kindly, would let this happen knowingly? I'm offended that you think I knew. Look, I just translate things. I'm not good with numbers. It wasn't my job to check all of it out. I wrote what he told me in your language. I didn't pay any particular attention to the details, except to see that I translated it without errors. I can't control price increases. Do you think I'm happy giving you this news?"

They were silent for several minutes. Rufus stood uncertainly. There was nothing more he could say. The stench from the improper body waste disposal area was beginning to make him ill.

"I can't change what has happened," he apologized. "But I will try to get him to improve these quarters. However, that may cost more, and from his mood this morning, I think he'll charge that to you as well."

"We must be permitted to dig a proper sanitation disposal area like we did at the other mine," Howard said with obvious irritation. "That will cost him nothing. If we request anything else, we want to know the cost in advance, and guaranteed in writing."

"As you wish," Rufus said, bowing low.

The portal banged open and the guard called to Rufus.

"I have to go now," Rufus said and walked out.

When the portal closed, Henry threw himself against it several times. He pounded it with his pods and shouted, "You can't keep us here!" over and over, although he knew no one outside was listening or cared. Still angry, he went to the far side of the chamber, where they had piled up all the debris and dirt. He picked up one rock or clod of dirt after another and threw them at the portal. Half way through the pile, Herbert joined him. When both had finished venting their anger, they sat down in the mess and stared at each other.

"Are you two calm enough to talk now?" Howard asked after several minutes of silence.

Henry nodded. "How can you be so calm, Howard?"

"If I were young like you, I would do the same. But my life is behind me. I look at things differently. Leave the mess for now. Come and meditate with me. Through the power of meditation, our cherished ones will sense our troubles. When we don't return tomorrow, Alyssa will demand an explanation. Our colony and our cherished ones will not abandon us. They will fight for our release."

*   *   *   *

Adeline sat in the shade of a small wood plant looking at the wooden bridge over the border stream. The bridge was only 150 f-units long, not as long as some she had seen images of that spanned much wider bodies of moving water, and the ants had built tunnels under many larger streams to connect various colonies. The banks sloped sharply but the water running at the bottom wasn't very wide. How could this stream bed be such a canyon separating her from the one she cherished?

Commander Ferdinand handed her a flask of water. "Here, Adeline, drink all you need. This is the hottest part of the day, but the traders should be here soon."

"Thank you. You know, I've never been on the surface before. I've lived my whole life underground."

"That's all right," he replied. "Less than one fourth of all ants ever go to the surface. You have a lot of company. We get used to the sun's heat in time."

"It certainly makes me appreciate you and the dairiers more," Adeline said.

He smiled at Adeline and turned to Alyssa, who was seated next to her along with most of South Harvester 45's Council. "Last time, when the traders came, they crossed the bridge to our side and unloaded the plastic from their roller carts so we could transfer it into our baskets. They handed us the communications last, and then ran off before we had a chance to respond. This time, we're ready. I have over one hundred guards hidden in the grass all around. As soon as they come across the bridge, the guards will surround them. That ought to persuade them to stay until you can read the official communications and respond."

"That's good," Alyssa said. "We are only missing two Council Members, both with family obligations. They said they will support any decision we make today."

Adeline thought about the brief message they had received the last time. "Work is proceeding very slowly. Be advised, it is unlikely that the tunnel will be finished by the end of the sixth time frame." In spite of it, she hoped that Henry and the others would be with the traders when they arrived. She had arranged for their mating ceremony to take place the following seventhday.

A guard reported to Commander Ferdinand that a look-out at the top of a wood plant had seen the traders coming. He was relieved to hear that there were only about fifty roach warriors.

"Hold the grassfrond high as they come across the bridge," Commander Ferdinand said. "Fifty of you move into position at our end of the bridge right behind them. Keep your grassfrond up. They are unlikely to attack when they see our superior numbers, but we want them to know we mean no harm."

Adeline reached for the water flask again, but her pod was shaking and she knocked it over. "I'm sorry," she stammered.

Alyssa put a reassuring pod on the back of her thorax. "Have courage, Adeline. Perhaps it will be good news."

Only a few ant guards stood in plain sight, holding a grassfrond. The traders hesitated and then moved forward. The warriors acknowledged the grassfrond and remained on their side of the bridge. The rolling carts rumbled across the bridge, pulled and pushed by several large roach workers. The ants watched from their hiding places and waited until the traders and rolling carts were off the bridge and closer to them.

Swiftly, a large group of fire ants moved onto the trail, blocking the way back to the bridge. A second group rose from the tall meadow grass beside the trail and surrounded the traders. Tension hung in the air, thick as honey, but the roach warriors remained in place.

Commander Ferdinand moved toward the lead trader and escorted Alyssa to meet him. She held up a piece of parchment and said, "Please, give me any official communications you are carrying," hoping he would guess her meaning.

The lead trader reached into his pod-held satchel and took out a sealed parchment. His antennae twitched quickly back and forth and his pod shook slightly. Commander Ferdinand sat down and gestured for the roach to do the same, hoping to relieve his fear. The roach glanced about and sat down. The other roaches followed his example.

Relieved that their intent was understood, Alyssa signaled to Adeline and the other Council Members. When they were seated beside her, she broke the seal and read the message:

> To South Harvester 45:
> Henry, Herbert, and Howard are all in good health.
> The tunnel is complete, but there is a more serious problem.Their living expenses and materials have run far over the agreed credit limit, even though the amount
> promised you was more than sufficient. That, and all
> the costs for their security, have the South East RoachControl Board very upset. The three have agreed to remain and work until the debt is paid. As ants who are known to honor all
> agreements, we know you will approve of this.
> Son of Sir Rudy, S.E.R.C.B. Member,
> translated by Rufus.

Under the translation, was a second piece of parchment with the original words in Roach.

"That's preposterous!" shouted the oldest Council Member. "No ant could possibly require that much credit for living expenses in this short a time! Even those few who have been cited for selfish use in all the antstory of our colony have come nowhere near that figure."

"I was there the day we made the agreement," Adeline put in. "Herbert sat there and pledged all of his share to the colony saying he didn't need much."

Alyssa shook her head. "I was hoping it wouldn't happen to us as it did to the other colonies where Rufus has been. I'm sure that if we looked at their copy of the agreement, we would find that the placement points are different, showing this huge amount in ours and much less in theirs. We were all so excited, we didn't pay attention to Master Andrea's desire to send it to the Intercolonial Council first. If we had, we would have known what happened in the other colonies. We could have checked it better for errors. What have I done to them?"

Adeline's mind reeled. She clenched her mandibles and forced herself to think rationally and remain in control. The discussion went on around her, how unfair it was, but their honor was being questioned.

Adeline took a deep breath and spoke with a sense of determination she had never experienced so strongly. "I won't allow this. They cannot keep Henry against my will. I didn't sign that agreement. I want him returned to me immediately. You should demand that Rufus return and explain this to us. Tell him to bring the original copy of the agreement in Roach and all their expense records. The contract specifically states that expense records would be provided. I demand to see them. Henry belongs to me. Our promise dates from before this agreement."

Commander Ferdinand looked at Adeline with complete respect and turned to Alyssa and the other Council Members. "She's right."

Alyssa nodded. "I doubt that Roacheria will honor our customs regarding that, given their past actions, but it is a bargaining tool we can certainly use to insist that they be returned to us. We constantly give in to Roacheria's demands. The time has come to make requests of our own. Hand me parchment and ink. I can state this quickly."

The document was signed by Alyssa, all the Council Members present, Adeline, and Commander Ferdinand.

"That ought to get their attention," Commander Ferdinand said as he signed it.

"I will send word of this to The Intercolonial Council as soon as we are back in the colony. I'm sure they will give their support," Alyssa concluded.

*   *   *   *

Rex scowled at Rufus. "Over one hundred fire ants detained my traders to give me this?"

"Yes, Sir. Peacefully, Sir."

"Well, what does it say?"

Rufus began to read his translation of the letter. "To the Son of Sir Rudy."

"They don't know my name, do they?" Rex interrupted.

"No, Sir, I've been most careful about that."

"Good. Continue."

Rufus read:

"We find it impossible to believe that three of our colony members could use the amount of credit stated in the agreement between us in so short a time. We demand that Rufus return to show us the original document in Roach. We wish to check for discrepancies between it and our copy, having been informed by the Intercolonial Council that Rufus has made serious mistakes before which have cost other colonies many thousands of credit units. We also demand that he bring copies of the expense reports and explain them in detail. Only if he can satisfy us will we continue to honor the agreement. In any case, Henry must be returned at once, as his Promised One has withdrawn her consent to his participation in this project. Sir Rudy was aware of Henry's obligation to another when he requested Henry. Your prompt reply will be appreciated."

Rufus stopped a moment and then said, "It's signed by Alyssa, their Council Chief, several Council Members, Adeline, and Commander Ferdinand, their fire ant commander."

"Who is Adeline? Wait, I know. How can a lowly female demand anything of me?"

Rufus explained. "Sir, she is Henry's Promised One. As I told you before, that means he has freely given himself to her as a mate. He allows her to control his life. A male ant always respects the wishes of his mate. I tried to explain that to your father. I told him that it was Adeline he had to convince, if he insisted on having Henry. She nodded her consent, but did not sign the contract. Under their law, she has every right to demand his return now."

Rex pounded his work surface with one front pod. "This isn't their law. It's my law and I own him now. She can't have him back. He's the most intelligent of the lot. My father could see that and so can I. You convinced them that the expense statements were correct and that they owed me labor. Go convince the other ants. Tell them we don't recognize any mating contract unless a physical union has taken place. It hasn't, has it?"

"No, Sir, but convincing the entire colony will be a bit more difficult than the three ants here. It wasn't hard for them to decide to stay with several of your security warriors standing there threatening them. I'll be by myself there with fire ants all around me, and they know about my other deals now."

"Judging by your past performances, I'd say you're up to the challenge," Rex said with a smile. "You've got two time frames before the traders' next trip to plan your story. That ought to give you plenty of time to make sure the expense reports are in order and dream up some new lies. I'll have one of my financial officers assist you with the documents. Meanwhile, we'll use that 'materials provided' phrase to charge them with the security expenses, and remind them that it doesn't say 'free of charge.' You know I'll make it worth your while."

"Yes, Sir,"Rufus said, backing out of Rex's chamber.

17.

*G*abriel knew something was terribly wrong. He did not know for certain why the ants had stayed beyond the end of the sixth time frame, but the look in their eyes and their drooping antennae said it was not voluntarily.

Rufus avoided Gabriel as much as possible. When they were together with the ants, which was only on firstday and fourthday of each quarter time frame, Rufus stuck to business. When Gabriel managed to be alone with Rufus he pressed for answers.

Rufus only repeated, "You're better off not knowing."

Gabriel wanted to ask Henry what was going on, but Henry's downhearted appearance prevented it. Gabriel had learned to respect their ways, and asking would definitely be personal. None of the words and phrases he knew how to say in Ant fit the circumstances. He tried to ask with his eyes and leave himself open in case Henry decided to tell him, since he could usually understand what they said.

What frustrated him the most was knowing that he couldn't do anything to improve their situation. Each time he approached their quarters at the Number 6 Mine, warriors guarding it turned him away. They had their orders; he was not to enter.

"Why am I not permitted to be with my instructors?" he asked Ganton.

"Things have changed. You have two work days each quarter time frame. That's enough." Ganton never made a direct threat, but Gabriel knew if he persisted, he was likely to suffer for it.

He tried to follow Rufus' advice but he couldn't. His conversations through Rufus during the third, fourth, and fifth time frames about life in an ant colony had changed him. Ignoring their plight was impossible. The memory of how elated he had felt the day Sir Rudy had offered him this "opportunity," and how willing he was to participate, filled him with shame.

Toward the end of the seventh time frame as he sat with them at lunch one fourthday, he noticed that the three of them had only water. He searched his mind for the Ant words he needed.

"Your food?" he finally managed.

Henry looked at him with more sorrow than Gabriel had ever seen in his life. "We are saving it for supper," was all Henry said.

Gabriel handed Henry part of his own lunch. Henry accepted it gratefully and divided it into portions to share with the others. Gabriel had heard that Rex had cut supplies to the shanty workers. Perhaps he had cut back their food ration as well. He handed Henry the rest of his lunch and said with poor pronunciation, "I'm sorry."

Henry shook his head. "It's not your fault. Thank you."

Gabriel took enough lunch for four each firstday and fourthday after that. It was the least he could do.

*   *   *   *

Late in the evening, around the middle of the eighth time frame, Gabriel answered a tapping at the portal of his domicile. Of all creatures, there stood Rufus.

Rufus stooped low and said, "Gabriel, I know I have insulted you many times, and you have every reason to hate me. You can say, 'I told you so,' but, please, don't. Right now, I need to talk to someone and you're the only one I can tell. I shouldn't even tell you. He's been paying me not to. I just can't do it any more."

Gabriel looked at him strangely and said, "Come in."

"No, not here. Come for a walk with me. I never thought I would need a friend, but I need one now."

"Wait a moment," Gabriel said.

He turned and walked over to his mate. "I have to go out for a while. It's about work. Don't worry. I won't have any ale. I promise. Don't wait up for me." He slid one front pod across the back of her thorax, up her head and to the tip of her antenna.

"Gabriel, what's wrong?" she asked.

"I think I'm about to find out," he said and left with Rufus.

They wandered up one lane and down another, while Rufus told Gabriel the whole ugly truth. Rufus told him about his first meeting with Sir Rudy, and how he had advised the now dead Board Member about how to word the contract to deceive the ants. He told Gabriel that he had given all the letters to Rex, and had been made to read many of them to him. He related the details of his meeting with Rex when the ants came into Roacheria after the second time frame to see about the letters, and how he had lied to pacify them.

He told how Rex had sent warriors to act as though they were protecting the ants on their return trip, even staging a fake attack, so the story would be more convincing. He told Gabriel how Rex had written the expense statements, and every other lie he had ever made up, including those he had told Gabriel.

Gabriel listened and said nothing. He was appalled by the depth of the deceit and the seriousness of the situation. They had walked near the trade and transport area of the city by this time. Rufus sat down on the ground with a sigh. Thunder rumbled faintly from a distant but towering summer storm cloud.

"Now, Rex is sending me back to South Harvester 45," Rufus said. "I'm supposed to convince them that those three owe him work. The problem is that the different colonies I have been in have all talked with each other. They have figured out how I cheated them. I hate to say it, but you were right. It's all caught up to me. I'm done for, Gabriel. What am I going to do?"

He continued before Gabriel could respond. "You know, I used to think the credit was enough. I could keep doing it for the credit and forget about them. Now I have more credit units than I know what to do with. Can you believe that? Curse Henry. Remember what he said that day? 'What would you do with more than you needed?' Curse him! He was right. They're all right. Their whole way of life is right and we're all wrong. The rotten timbers in the tunnel of my life are breaking; it's going to collapse. I can't change the reality we live in. I can't stop what he's going to do to them."

"You might try telling the truth when you go to South Harvester 45. Ants seem to be understanding and forgiving creatures."

"Oh, sure," Rufus said sarcastically. "If I do that, I'll have ants from five colonies lined up for d-units for the chance to extinguish me. If I fail to convince them, Rex will see to it that I end up in the mantis compound. This will probably end up in a war. I'm dead either way. I wonder which is worse, being eaten by a mantis or feeling the venom in a fire ant's sting."

"Maybe we could set them free."

Rufus laughed. "Right. We'll walk up to all Rex's security warriors and say, 'Please, unlock the portal,' then we'll run away with them. Tell me another joke."

Thunder rumbled again, louder and closer this time. Rufus got up and began walking. Gabriel followed him.

"I never thought I would hear myself say this," Gabriel offered, "but maybe you could think of a lie for their colony that would satisfy them for a while. Then we would have more time to think of a way out of this."

"That's what I've been trying to do for the last six quarter time frames. Everything I think of sounds worse."

They wandered ever closer to the Trade and Transportation Center and Rufus told Gabriel the stories he had thought of. "You're right," Gabriel said. "Those are pretty bad excuses. They wouldn't fool a nymph."

They stopped in the shadows at the edge of the wide path leading from the Trade Center. Even this late at night, workers were there loading huge roller carts with plastic, bound for various communities of Organized Roacheria.

"My life was so much simpler when I worked there. I wish those ants had left me for dead. I wouldn't be in this mess now," he said, turning toward Gabriel and looking directly at him. Gabriel saw more anguish in his eyes than he had thought possible.

Rufus pointed to a roller cart approaching them and said slowly, "It didn't feel so bad, you know, being crushed. There was hardly any pain until later. It kind of numbs you, the first crack does."

"Rufus, we can think of something. I'm sure we can."

"No, Gabriel, I can't. You live with it. I can't any more. I'll be the one to choose my fate. Tell my son to learn to speak Ant. Maybe someday he can apologize for me."

Before Gabriel could stop Rufus, he bolted out of the shadows and threw himself beneath a heavily loaded, oncoming roller cart. The workers on the pulling end cried out to him and tried to stop, but it was too late. A sickening crackling sound reached Gabriel's ears. Rufus was no more. Retching inside, Gabriel fled before anyone saw him.

*   *   *   *

The thunder awakened Henry from his fitful sleep. He hoped that this time it would bring sky water to cool them. Every day, the sun beat down on the metal roof raising the temperature of their quarters like the inside of a cooking box. The three of them tried to stay within the cool tunnels of the mine as long as they could each day. It wasn't too difficult given the long h-units they were now expected to work.

Rex sent them plenty of water, but only eight weight units of seeds each quarter time frame and no other kind of food. They ate sparingly in the morning and saved the rest of each day's portion for evening, so that they were not kept awake by hunger pangs as well as heat. The food Gabriel gave them helped some. Once in a while one of the workers gave them some food, but they didn't seem to have much either.

Herbert had found some fungus growing inside the mine tunnel. He had brought some of it to their quarters and was trying to start a fungus patch in the pile of dirt that still remained in one corner of their quarters. They kept it moist with drinking water and fertilized it sparingly with their own body waste, as Herbert had been taught to do when he had worked in South Harvester 45's fungus gardens during his job exploration training. But the heat prevented it from growing well. It would be quite a while before it would add an appreciable amount to their food supply.

The thunder grew louder. Henry raised his head and looked around. Herbert and Howard seemed to be sleeping soundly, so he lifted his pods in meditation and concentrated his thoughts on Adeline. His uplifted thoughts were disturbed by the sound of voices outside the portal. The voices were not loud, but it was definitely an argument. He thought he recognized Gabriel's voice and moved over to the portal to hear better. The argument continued.

Thunder crashed several times in rapid succession and he heard the patter of sky water on the metal overhead. The portal opened. Gabriel was shoved in and the portal slammed again.

"What's going on?" Howard asked sleepily.

"Gabriel is here," Henry said, turning on a lamp.

He turned to Gabriel, who was shaking all over. He spoke very slowly, so Gabriel would understand. "Gabriel, what is wrong?"

Gabriel's antennae drooped and he groaned. "All things wrong," he said in barely understandable Ant before breaking down completely.

While the sky water pounded on the roof above, Henry comforted the mournful roach. He stroked Gabriel's back and antennae, hoping to soothe him enough to find out what was troubling him so much that he had come to them in the middle of the night.

Gabriel finally stopped shaking and looked up at them. Howard held out a cup of water. He accepted it and said, "Please, parchment and ink."

While Herbert reached for some, they moved over to the eating surface. Gabriel sighed and began to draw an image of Rufus on the ground in front of the roller cart. "Rufus dead," he said.

The three ants stared at the picture.

"When?" asked Henry.

"Tonight," replied Gabriel.

"An accident?"

Gabriel shook his head. He did not know how he could possibly explain it all, but he had to try. "You here," he began. "All wrong. Rufus say you not leave here, ever. He make you stay. Not go home. All wrong. Rufus say maybe . . ." He stopped because he didn't know the Ant words for war or fight. He quickly drew roach warriors and fire ants, battle ready. "No, no, wrong. A different answer, please."

Henry looked at Gabriel and at the drawing and thought about the events of the last two time frames. He spoke slowly, "Gabriel, are you saying that Rufus killed himself because of what Sir Rudy's son is doing in keeping us here?"

Gabriel nodded.

"But we have to stay, because of the credit."

Gabriel shook his antennae. "No. Wrong. Rufus dead for what he did to you."

"But it is not Rufus' fault. He doesn't set the prices. What do you mean?"

Gabriel gave up. There was no way that he could explain about the deceit. He might as well let them believe there was something good about Rufus and lay the blame where it belonged. "Rufus know you never go home. So sad, so sorry. He tell me. He made himself dead not to face you. Sir Rudy's son, not good."

"Do you mean that Sir Rudy's son plans to keep us here as prisoners forever?"

Gabriel nodded.

Howard put one front pod on Gabriel's back. "Is everyone here treated like we are?"

Gabriel nodded.

"Those who live there," Howard asked, pointing in the direction of the worker shanties on the far side of the mine pit, "does he make them stay there?"

"Yes," Gabriel said, lowering his antennae in shame. He took parchment again and drew the Banner Of Roacheria. Then he drew a large roach with several Board Ornaments around his head with his back pods on the head of a smaller roach.

He pointed to the one arrow. "Credit," he said. He pointed to the second and the ornaments. "Power," he said. "Us," he said, pointing to the roach being stepped on, and pointing to the back of his own head. "Life here, not good."

"Has he done that to you?" Howard asked.

"Yes."

Howard spoke to Henry and Herbert. "I didn't want to believe my own eyes. I think I have seen him. The other day at lunch time, I was standing just inside the tunnel entrance. On the opposite rim, I saw a young male roach wearing several of those ornaments. Ganton was with him. Two of the warriors forcefully brought one of the workers before him. Even at that distance, their voices rang with anger. The young male with the ornaments beat on the worker mercilessly, then pushed him over the rim. He tumbled down the slope and lay still. The other workers did not go near the injured one until Ganton and the young male left. Then they went over and took care of him."

Howard turned back to Gabriel and spoke slowly. "Will he hurt you if he knows you came here? Will that warrior," he pointed toward the portal, "tell him?"

"Yes, but I give warrior credit. Not tell then. You think about problem. I think about problem. We find answer. You be free. Not this answer," he said, pointing to his picture of the battle scene once more.

He walked toward the portal and tapped lightly. "I go now. Day soon." It opened slightly and he disappeared into the night. The three ants sat down to ponder his news.

Henry spoke first. "I've had a bad feeling ever since we came to this mine. I just couldn't put it into words, and I couldn't admit to myself that it was possible. We should have realized it when he said there wouldn't be any letters. We should have seen it when the warriors here forced us in. I'm so numb right now I can't even be angry."

"How could Rufus lie to us so completely?" Herbert asked.

"Maybe he didn't know," Howard replied. "Remember what he said that day about the expense reports? He did as he was told and translated things. Nobody could be as cheerful as he was in the middle of lying."

"I think he knew part of it," Henry put in. "Because his mood changed during the sixth time frame. Didn't you see how he avoided us? He wouldn't let Gabriel ask things any more. He talked less and he wasn't so cheerful. I think when he found out, he felt so bad about it that he tried to avoid telling us until he couldn't put it off. Remember how agitated he was that day? He's hardly been around since then."

Howard said, "I think you're right, Henry. And maybe he was afraid of Sir Rudy's son. He and Gabriel, and all those workers are prisoners too. We're locked in physically, but our minds and hearts are free. We know our colony will fight for us. Who will fight for them? They must have no hope at all. That's even worse."

Herbert looked up at the ceiling. "Maybe we could push up on that metal sheet and wedge some rocks into the crack. We could do a little each night, and when the crack is large enough we could crawl out and escape."

Henry climbed on top of Herbert. He could reach the roof slab but could not push up with enough force to lift it.

"It's not so thick," Henry observed. "I've lifted things heavier than that before."

"Yes, but you had a firm surface under you, and you were in good health," replied Howard. "We've lost strength because we're not getting enough food."

Henry had another idea. "Suppose we sabotaged the working tunnel. We could set up a collapse with ourselves on the inside. I don't think it's that many f-units between this working level and the abandoned one above, and they haven't collapsed those entrances yet. We could dig our way upward, and escape through the other tunnels. They'd think we were trapped and wouldn't be looking for us to get away. By the time they redug it, we'd be long gone."

"How would we know which way to go across open surface to find our way home? And what about the bandits and renegades?" Herbert asked.

Henry sighed. He knew how to get back to the Number 1 Mine, but he couldn't remember anything beyond that. "Maybe there really aren't all that many bandits. Maybe Rufus was told to tell us that too, so we wouldn't think about trying to escape. Gabriel might be able to draw us a location chart."

"This idea has many dangers, to us and to the roach workers," Howard said. "We can't risk any of their lives if we decide it's the only way. We'll have to plan it very carefully and not be hasty, or we'll lose our own lives in the effort. I think we can begin to look for likely areas though. They are used to us moving about the tunnel inspecting and measuring, especially when Gabriel is here. Henry, next time he comes and you're going over charts, see if you can make him understand what we're thinking. Maybe you can get into that upper tunnel and have a look around. Try to make definite measurements so we can calculate things as exactly as possible."

18.

*T*he following fourthday, Gabriel and Henry sat hunched over their parchments, drawing furiously, and muttering to each other. Gabriel had a long discussion with the overseer, and was finally granted permission to take Henry into the abandoned tunnel above them. They had gone only a short way in when, to Henry's dismay, they found it was blocked with debris.

They returned to the overseer and Gabriel talked with him. He then returned to Henry and began to draw a chart Henry realized was fake. Henry looked at him curiously.

Gabriel tugged at his mid-right pod. "Look . . . busy," he said awkwardly. He continued to work at the fake chart and drew something else below it, which looked to Henry like a diagram of what they had seen in the upper tunnel. Gabriel whispered an Ant word now and then when he knew it, drew arrows and several pictures. He kept covering one parchment with another. Finally, he took a clean parchment, drew a legitimate chart, and calculations on it.

"Keep these, not him see, letter on firstday," he whispered, pushing all the drawings at Henry. He rose and gave the last one to the overseer. Then he stooped low in humility and left the mine area.

The others looked at Henry with anticipation. "No now,"he said.

*   *   *   *

At the end of his work day, Gabriel went to the Communications Center. Although it was very crowded, he did not recognize anyone from either of Rex's mines. He straightened up as much as he could and approached the box rental clerk.

Trying to look important, he said, "I'm here visiting from a distant community down the coast from Sea Edge. I'm on assignment as an aid to our representative on the South East Roach Control Board. I must have a box for his letters."

"I need authorization from your representative,"the clerk replied.

Gabriel's antennae twitched. He searched through his satchel for something that didn't exist, and then looked helplessly at the clerk. "I've . . . I've lost it. Oh, what am I going to do? He'll . . . He'll . . . Oh, what he'll do to me if I don't . . . Please, can't you just rent the box? I've got all this credit he sent with me."

Gabriel was shaking. If he got caught in this, his fate would be far worse than Rufus', and he suddenly appreciated that pathetic creature's ability to lie so convincingly. He had never dreamed that an authorization would be required.

"What's it like working for a Board Member?"the clerk asked.

"It's a living. You know, run here, run there, work like crazy to please them and still get stepped on,"Gabriel said.

The clerk sighed. "I was afraid so. I noticed the dent behind your head. Guess I haven't got it so bad. All right, here," he said, handing Gabriel the porper form.

Gabriel filled it out, listing the name as Sir Gabriel, and paid box rent for three time frames in advance. He handed the credit and the form to the clerk, and held out a little more credit to buy his silence.

The clerk looked at Gabriel and at the extra credit. "Keep it," he said. "Sir Gabriel will probably hold you accountable for the hundredth part of a unit."

Gabriel sighed with obvious relief. "Thank you."

He hurried away for the Communications Center, losing himself in the crowd, and returned home to begin work on the rest of his plan.

*   *   *   *

Henry, Howard, and Herbert looked at Gabriel's many drawings. Henry went over their "conversation" in detail.

"We can't dig upward to the next level. It's farther between the layers than I thought. Also, there is a collapsed area inside the entrance. Gabriel tried to find out when it had happened and how big the collapse was, but this overseer is new and didn't know. I got the impression that he didn't like Gabriel asking so many questions. Even if we took all the food we are given for a quarter time frame, and as much water as our flasks would hold, we might die before we dug our way free."

"So much for escape," sighed Herbert.

Henry continued. "Gabriel has another idea, but it's very risky for him. I understood from this," he said, pointing to another of Gabriel's drawings, "that he can conceal a letter from us to the colony by burying it in the next plastic shipment, which is next secondday. Apparently, Rufus was supposed to go and tell our Council some reason why we are not going home. Gabriel tried to tell me something about our colony demanding our return and threatening to send fire ants to rescue us. He is desperate to prevent a violent conflict, but still wants to free us."

"Is this drawing supposed to be Adeline?" Howard asked.

"Yes, he kept saying, 'You go cherish Adeline,' to me. I think he feels that if we could get a letter to the colony telling what is really going on here, they might be able to find a way to get us home without a war. I'm to give him the letter mixed in with a lot of tunnel charts when he comes on firstday."

"You said this was risky for Gabriel. Why?" asked Herbert.

Henry sighed and took out one last drawing. "If he is caught helping us, he will be condemned for treason. Here, if you are condemned for a violent crime or for treason, they put you in a walled area where they keep mantises captive and hungry."

"Oh, Creator Spirit," Howard sighed. "How can such cruelty exist in an intelligent civilization?"

Henry went on. "If there is a war over us, it will not be Sir Rudy's son and the other Board Members who will suffer. It will be the innocent and those they call 'lowest of the low', and creatures like Gabriel, and these workers we see every day, who struggle to survive in this terrible place. Please meditate with me, because I don't know how I will say this in my letter to Adeline."

*   *   *   *

Midafternoon came and the traders had not arrived. Once again, Adeline sat in the shade of the wood plants not far from the border bridge. Again, Alyssa and the Council Members sat with her. Her pods shook and her antennae twitched uncontrollably.

"I can't stand this waiting much longer. Why aren't they here yet?" she asked for the twentieth time.

She felt Alyssa's comforting pods surround her, gave in, and leaned against her. Gently, Alyssa stroked her body with her middle pods. With an even softer touch, she stroked Adeline's antennae until she was calm.

"We don't know why they are so late, but we will all stay here until they come. Commander Ferdinand is ready with all the guards, like last time. We will make them stay and wait for our reply."

Adeline straightened up. "I'm sorry I keep losing control of myself. Waiting and waiting and not knowing is so hard. I go to work every morning and I try to function. Sometimes it seems like my co-workers take as much care of me as they do the larvae. That's what I feel like, a helpless larva. I took some time off and that was even worse. Do you know how many times I cleaned our domicile crying in frustration?"

"Hopefully, today will be the end of your waiting," Alyssa replied. "At any rate, don't apologize for your behavior. Howard's daughter and Herbert's parents are going through the same thing, to such a degree that they feel unable to participate in any of this. You are strong, Adeline, and all of us will give you even more strength."

Commander Ferdinand interrupted them. "The traders are finally approaching. Our lookout could not see Henry, Howard, or Herbert with them, and they have at least one hundred warriors. Please, for your safety, stay here until I signal. Adeline, I know how much being here means to you. Climb this wood plant. You will be able to see and hear if you remain very quiet."

"I'll climb it with you," Alyssa offered.

When they reached the bridge, the trading party stopped. The warriors formed ranks along the bank, standing twenty wide and six deep on either side of the bridge, ready to swoop down the bank and up the ants' side. Slowly, one roach stepped onto the bridge, walked to the middle and stopped.

He held a thick packet before him and shouted in Ant. "I will come no closer. I know many fire ants are hidden in the grass. If you want these documents, come and get them."

Commander Ferdinand turned to the closest guard. "Pass the word to stay back unless I signal." He took up the grassfrond of peace and walked onto the bridge.

When he reached the center, he faced the roach standing there and said, "I am Commander Ferdinand. I'm glad to have an interpreter this time. It's not our intent to hurt anyone. A lack of communication is much of this problem. The traders don't wait for us to respond, and we can't delay this another two time frames. If you don't want to cross the bridge, fine. Sit and talk with me here."

The roach sat down. "Here are the documents you requested."

"Where is Rufus?"

"Rufus will never come here again for fear of you. Your previous letter accused him falsely of errors. The documents I handed you will prove our position beyond any doubt. You will see that Rufus' translations are accurate. Our Board can't help it if you don't read a contract carefully and ask enough questions before signing it. It's all there. Perhaps this time you should study it better. Take the next two time frames. That ought to give you enough time to see our position for yourselves."

"Remain here and let me take this to our Council Chief. She is here and ready to look at this now." Commander Ferdinand offered. "If it will make you more comfortable, I will have my guards withdraw. You may do the same with your warriors. The sight of them there, ready to swarm across the water makes us nervous too."

"No, I was instructed to leave these with you. If you take the time you should, it will be many days. It took Rufus all this time to prepare these for you. All of Roacheria is insulted by your accusations. You judge with no real idea of living expenses in Roacheria."

He gestured toward the roller carts and continued. "The traders have been told to leave the roller carts here in the middle of the bridge. As a sign of our good faith, we will leave the roller carts with you until we return in two time frames. We will not collect the fees for this delivery.

You may include it at the end of the tenth time frame when your harvest is complete."

"In the mean time, what about our colony members? It is wrong of you to hold them against their will."

"They have agreed to stay. You are the problem. As for the one who is promised, our law does not recognize a mating contract until after physical union. We will not recognize her claim on him. He stays with the other two. You will understand when you study the documents."

Before Commander Ferdinand could reply, he said, "Don't send any of your special envoys onto our surface, as you did several time frames ago. We will consider any entrance into our territory a hostile act. I have nothing more to say." He turned and walked back to the Roacherian side of the stream. The traders, pushing only, and remaining behind their loads, delivered the roller carts to the middle of the bridge. Then the traders and the warriors retreated down the trail into Roacheria.

Commander Ferdinand handed the packet to Alyssa. "I'm sorry. If I had anticipated this, you could have spent this day in the comfort of the colony."

"It's all right," Alyssa replied. "I have no desire to engage in battle when our position may be unclear. We'll study these carefully."

"May I sit with you when you do?" Adeline asked.

"Of course."

It was late afternoon by the time Adeline and the others returned to the colony. The packet contained dozens of documents. They were so mixed up that it took them another h-unit to sort the copies written in Roach from those in Ant. Then they found they did not know which parchment in Ant went with what one in Roach, so they could begin to examine the numbers. By the time they found the code, a tiny number embedded in the text of each bottom line, it was well into the evening and all of them were exhausted.

The following morning they began to examine those written in Ant. Only six of them listed the expenses directly. The rest seemed to be a long, tedious explanation of Roacherian pricing methods and were signed, "Chief Provisions Manager for Sir Rudy's Son." Over and over they read, "Provided does not mean free of charge."

They were working on totalling the amount Roacheria claimed the three ants owed, when the Colony Commodities Manager entered the chamber.

"Please excuse the interruption, but a worker found this buried in one of the containers of plastic we received yesterday. It has Adeline's name and domicile location on it, so I came right away."

Adeline took it from him. The chamber was silent as she read the letter:

"My most cherished Adeline,

"If your are reading these words, it is because Gabriel has risked his life to get them to you. Since I have been given none of the letters I know you must have written in the beginning, I assume that you received none of mine. After the third time frame, we were told not to write any more.

"I have no idea what you or anyone in the colony knows of our plight, so I will sum it up briefly. We were attacked by renegades on the first day. Sir Rudy was brutally murdered. We were rescued by Sir Rudy's personal warriors and brought to his mine. Our living quarters were quite bad, but we were safe from further attack and were treated decently. We began to build the tunnel and train Gabriel and a crew of workers as we had been hired to do.

"We finished the tunnel at the first mine half a time frame before our contract ended and were moved to a different mine. Since then, we have been treated abominably.

"Sir Rudy's son, who now controls our lives, is in Gabriel's broken Ant, 'Not good.' Each time frame we adjusted our requests to stay within our credit limit, but no matter what we did, we were charged with more, and charged for things we had assumed would be given to us. No ant should ever again trust any roach's word, especially not the phrase, 'will be provided.' That has become our trap.

No matter what we do here, we will never earn enough to cover the expenses. We will never be free.

"Several days ago, Gabriel came to us in the night and told us with the few Ant words he knows and many pictures, that Rufus had killed himself when he realized what Sir Rudy's son was doing. Understanding our way of life, Rufus apparently could not live with the guilt he felt for being part of it. The three of us truly believe that he only translated what he was told and had no knowledge of anything more. Also, we have come to know that he would have been severely punished if he did not do exactly as he was told. We have witnessed some of their abuse.

"We are always locked in and guarded to prevent our escape. He does not give us enough food now, and we are losing body mass and strength. Our quarters are like a cooking box in this season. When winter comes, we will be equally cold and suffer even more. If our food supply is not increased, we will waste away soon after the new season cycle begins.

"Please, believe that all I ever wanted was to make you happy and I have failed miserably. Forgive me for all the pain I have caused as you waited for me. Every fiber of my being is wretched when I realize that I will never see you again. Many times, I have wished that we had shared our gift of life that last day. But I am glad we didn't, because in time your feelings of hurt, anger, and grief will ease. Then you will be able to find the joy and fulfillment with another that I will never be able to give to you. My heart is so heavy as I write this, that it is hard to continue. You should release yourself from our promise and abandon me.

"We have meditated many h-units, and have decided that, if the sorrow we feel at this decision is the tiniest fraction of the sorrow that will be felt by hundreds of individuals and families if the colony sends fire ants to fight to free us; then we do not want you to fight a war for our sake. Sir Rudy's son and the other members of the

S.E.R.C.B. will not be the ones who will suffer if there is war. It will be the innocent who endure slavery here as we

do, under the tyranny of a horribly unjust system, and many ants who will die in battle, leaving their families to grieve. If the three of us must sacrifice ourselves to prevent that, then so be it. Our lives will have gone for what we believe and our essences will be forever at peace.

"I remain forever, faithfully, your Henry."

When she finished it she stared at them and then began shouting, **"No! No! No!"** She ran from the chamber. Blinded by churning emotions, Adeline dashed up one tunnel and down another.

＊   ＊   ＊   ＊

When Adeline awoke several h-units later, she vaguely remembered someone holding her down and giving her an injection. Her eyes opened to see her sister sitting beside her sleep cushion.

She cried, "What have I done?"

Deanna stroked her, "I thought I would go insane when Dean was killed. You were there for me. Now I'm here for you."

"I never wanted anyone else, Deanna. Do you ever want someone else?"

"Not right now. But someday, I might meet someone who has lost his mate, too, and we might raise our families together."

"I never cherished anyone else. I don't think I ever can. Why would Henry write that to me when he knows we'll all fight for them? I wish we'd gone ahead and given ourselves to each other. We talked about it the day before he left. At least I'd have something of him."

"No, Adeline, under the circumstances, he's done the kindest, most cherishing thing he could. He and the others are making the ultimate sacrifice so that many families don't feel as you do now. It will be a long time before you can accept it. Right now, what you feel is worse than the grief I felt. At least I could cover Dean and make his memorial marker."

"Excuse me," Adeline's father entered the chamber. "Alyssa is here."

Adeline rose. Alyssa embraced her. "Have hope, Adeline. I think we've found a way. The Council will offer to buy them back. We will send all the credit they demand, even if we think they are wrong. Commander

Ferdinand thinks he has figured out the meaning of the second piece of parchment."

"What second piece of parchment?" asked the bewildered Adeline.

"After you left the council chamber yesterday, another letter fell from behind it. It was from Gabriel, their engineer. He has drawn pictured instructions for you to write back. It's obvious that Henry didn't know that Gabriel had found a way for you to send a letter back to him."

19.

*T*he Supreme Executor of the S.E.R.C.B. drew Rex aside at one of their regular meetings during the ninth time frame. "Some of us are a little nervous about the number of fire ants stationed on The Colonies' side of the bridge. What's going on, Young Sir Rex?"

"I've delayed sending their engineers back," Rex replied. "Don't worry about it. I've got the legal end of it well sealed in our favor."

"Did you ever get any information about why your interpreter threw himself beneath that roller cart?"

"No. Nobody in the trade center that night knew who he was. I talked to his mate myself. She was hysterical. I could tell she knew nothing. I think he lost his objectivity. He was worried about going back to South Harvester 45. It's just as well. If he'd gone back acting like that, he might have broken down and betrayed us all. Maybe he decided the roller cart was better than the mantis compound. At this point I'm better off without him."

"How did you fix it with the ants?"

"I let them know that things are not provided free of charge."

The Supreme Executor laughed and said, "Your father would be proud of you."

*   *   *   *

Henry drank thirstily from the flask. "When will the days begin to get cooler, Howard?"

"What time frame is it? I'm beginning to lose track."

"It's the last day of the ninth time frame."

"If I remember correctly, it should begin to cool down before the end of the tenth time frame," Howard answered.

"It's cooled enough for our fungus patch to produce a little," Herbert added. "Here, our first home grown meal." He handed them each a fair sized piece of fungus.

"How often do you think we'll be able to eat it?" Henry asked.

"About twice a quarter time frame, for now. Hopefully, every day later on," Herbert replied. "It'll make up for the cut from eight to seven weight units of seeds. We can eat our share of seeds for breakfast and have fungus for supper."

"I don't know why we bother," Henry said. "Sometimes, I think it would be easier to pull one of those timbers at the entrance down on myself and finish it."

Howard moved over to Henry and encircled him with his appendages. He stroked Henry a long time. "Our lives are not ours to take. Only Essence can give and take life. These creatures own our bodies, but they can never own our essences. Don't give in to despair, Henry. We must preserve our dignity. The day we lower ourselves to their level, we will be lost for all time. But if we hold on to ourselves and do what is right, even if we must die for what we believe, then our essences will know peace. Even in this place, the example we set is important. More and more lately, I have seen the roach workers help each other. It used to be only Gabriel who brought us extra food. Now, three of the others take turns giving us a little lunch. If we plant in them the tiniest idea that there is a better way, our lives have not been lived in vain."

Eyes filled with despair, Henry said, "I think I'll try to make Gabriel understand about my journal the next time we see him, and trust him to do with it what he thinks is right."

*   *   *   *

Commander Ferdinand leaned over Adeline. "Be sure you copy the symbols exactly on the outside. I think Gabriel has set this up so that it looks like it's for some Board Member. If it's not perfect, we may endanger him as well as Henry and the others."

"Do you think this looks right? I wish the parchment were thin enough to see his symbols through it. Then I could trace it," she said, looking at him for approval.

"I don't think I could do better. Gabriel's drawings show that we should put this one in among our letters to The Board and Sir Rudy's son, whatever his name is. I wish they would tell us."

"Why don't they?" Adeline asked.

"Supposedly, saying 'Sir Rudy's son' has to do with showing respect for someone of greatness who has died. Personally, I think they don't want us to know who to blame," Commander Ferdinand replied.

"I wrote this letter, too. I hope it's all right. It's my own personal appeal to him."

"I'm sure it can't hurt," he said, putting her letter to Sir Rudy's son with The Council's letter to him and burying the one to Gabriel in the middle of the pile of communications to The Board. "These will go with the trade goods from the fall harvest we have ready to send to Roacheria tomorrow morning. Let's lift up our thoughts that our offer is accepted, because if it isn't, we will prepare for war, and I'll be the first one across that bridge. I don't care how many of their warriors face me."

He put his front pods on the back of Adeline's thorax and continued. "All of us lift up our thoughts for them every day, and for you and Howard's and Herbert's families. I can't imagine how difficult it is for you, and you must wait another two time frames to see if our offer is accepted."

"I've reached the point where I just try to get through each day as it comes. I try not to think about things much," she said.

*   *   *   *

Rex sat behind his work surface, listening to his new interpreter translate South Harvester 45's reply.

"To Sir Rudy's son,

"After much study and discussion of the documents you sent, we make this offer. We do not agree with the amount, or to your demand of payment for things we assumed would be provided without charge. We will be all the wiser next time. Never again will we allow ourselves to be tricked in this way. However, even though we do not agree, we offer you the full amount of credit owed, if you will return our colony members to us with the next trade trip. You should also be aware that we are quite prepared to fight for their release. South Harvester Colony 45 Council, and Alyssa, Council Chief."

Sir Rex stifled his laughter in front of this new interpreter. After nearly a season cycle of the ants' services for next to no cost, they were now offering to buy them back! Why hadn't someone thought of doing this ages ago? It was too good an idea, that was why. It took someone as crafty as he to come up with it.

The interpreter broke into his thoughts. "Sir, there is another letter here."

"What?"

"It's also to you, Sir. Shall I open it?"

"Yes."

The interpreter broke the seal, looked at it for a few minutes, and then read,

"Son of Sir Rudy,

"I would prefer to use your name, but since I do not know it, I cannot. Since you have lost your father, you must know the intense pain of separation from someone you care deeply about. You must know my pain. I appeal to you, in the name of everything decent and right, return Henry to me, or at least allow me to join him, if you refuse our colony's offer. I will give myself to you and work beside him to help pay off this debt, if you will accept me. Respectfully, Adeline."

Rex controlled his desire to roll on the floor laughing, for he did still pretend to grieve. Instead, he said in a tone somewhere between grief and sarcasm, "Just what I need, a mated pair of ants raising a bunch of larvae. I'll send for you half way through the twelfth time frame to translate my reply. Take the bill for your services to my financial records keeper. He'll see to it that you get paid. You are excused."

The interpreter nodded and left. Alone, Rex laughed until his muscles ached.

*   *   *   *

Gabriel waited until the day after he knew the traders had returned from South Harvester 45, before going to the communications box he had rented. Over the last two time frames he had sent several letters to himself as, "Sir Gabriel, S.E.R.C.B.," using various script styles, so the workers there would get used to seeing him and think he really was an aide to a Board Member from a distant community.

As he opened his box and removed Adeline's long awaited letter, the clerk he had seen the first day approached him. "Somebody sure can't write well. That script looks like some nymph did it."

Gabriel twitched. "It's probably from Sir Gabriel's son. He is nine season cycles old and just started to learn to write. Oh, I won't be coming any more. He's got a permanent domicile here now, and is going to pay to have letters taken directly there." He said it without hesitating! Was this how Rufus had started? Little necessary lies, that grew into bigger ones as the occasion called for it?

Gabriel walked slowly from the Communications Center and then ran, stuffing Adeline's precious letter into his satchel with all his tunnel charts. As he got closer to the Number 1 Mine, he slowed down and thought about what he would say to Rex. He had not been allowed contact with the ants for some time. Rex insisted that he work on his own. When he could, he had slipped some of the workers a little extra credit, telling them to buy food and give it to the ants. He hoped they did.

He knew he would have to grovel to get to see Henry. Although he hated it, it didn't seem so bad when it was for them. There was a certain satisfaction in humbling himself before Rex, knowing it was fake, and getting the best of him even in that small way. Strangely, he felt better about himself when he did something for the ants.

"Gabriel, don't knock right now," warned the female receiving clerk. "Ganton's in there. Sir Rex told me not to interrupt."

"I'll wait," he said, moving right up to the door. He pressed his head and antennae to the wood and listened.

"Are you crazy?" hissed the clerk.

He waved one pod at her to be quiet and ignore him.

"They are actually offering to buy them?" Gabriel heard Ganton say.

"Yes, it's hard to believe they're that stupid and gullible, isn't it?"

"I assume you'll accept their offer."

"And have them go back and tell the rest of their colony the truth about their time here? No, thank you. I have a better idea. At the end of the twelfth time frame, I'll send that interpreter again, with only a few of my warriors, and you. He'll them we're so sorry, their engineers tried to do another of those controlled collapses and it went wrong. They got caught up in it. In my sorrow, I'll forgive the debt, and they are mine for life."

Gabriel could hear them laughing. "My compliments to your cleverness," he heard Ganton say. "What if they ask for the bodies?"

Rex hesitated a moment. "Gabriel is well trained, so I don't need them. I'll quit feeding them. Then when we return their bodies, after supposedly digging them out, they'll look like they've been buried in debris. We could add a fracture or two if needed."

Gabriel left the portal and hurried to the male sanitation area where he vomited. He cleaned up after himself, bathed with cool water and sipped some. Having regained his composure, he returned and rested his abdomen on the bench reserved for those waiting to see Rex, determined to stop Rex's plan.

The clerk looked at him strangely. "Ganton's gone. Shall I announce you?"

He nodded.

The clerk entered Rex's chamber and returned. "He will see you."

Gabriel entered slowly and prostrated himself before Rex.

"Rise. What is it you want, Gabriel?"

"Sir, I request most humbly to see Henry. I am preparing many problem charts for the time when your cousin and whomever else you choose for me to train will arrive. I want to train them well, and I would like to be sure that I have prepared these problems correctly and have the right answers myself."

"I don't have an interpreter for you," Rex said.

"I won't need one, Sir. Henry and I point at the numbers and problems and nod or shake our heads. We draw diagrams. Sir, I beg most humbly. I feel it is very important that I give proper training to others.

Please, allow me to work with him on these training materials." He took some of the charts from his satchel and held them up.

Rex tapped his back pod on the floor. Gabriel prostrated himself again and waited for whatever might come.

After several minutes of silence, Rex said, "I will give you one day. Make sure you take everything you want him to check, because it will be the last time. You may go next firstday. That will give you a little more time to prepare. You may rise and go."

"Thank you, Sir," Gabriel said, backing slowly out of the chamber.

*   *   *   *

Henry turned around at the sound of Gabriel's voice. His first thought was to clasp both front pods in friendship, but a warning look in Gabriel's eye, and the sight of Ganton standing beside Gabriel stopped him. Gabriel held out a thick stack of parchment, saying in Roach, "Please, check these charts with me."

"Check charts" was the only phrase Henry knew in Roach. He stepped away from the work area and reached out for the charts. Guessing that they were not free to speak, he concerned himself with the numbers, wondering what was going on. He reached for his sliding bead calculator and realized he had left it in their quarters, thinking he would not need it that day. Gabriel looked at him quizzically.

"I don't have my sliding bead calculator," he said, making a gesture to indicate the device.

Gabriel smiled, as if this were a bit of luck. Then he rose and moved toward Ganton. They spoke back and forth for several minutes, Ganton's voice expressing irritation. Gabriel bowed low, and his voice seemed to beg. Ganton finally waved a pod at Gabriel and sighed. Gabriel motioned to Henry and began to walk toward the entrance of the mine.

Bewildered, Henry followed Gabriel and Ganton up the path to the mine rim and over to the ants' quarters. Ganton spoke to the warrior guarding the door, then gestured to Gabriel and Henry to enter. When the portal had slammed behind them, Gabriel sighed with relief and embraced Henry.

He whispered, "We talk now."

"Gabriel, what's going on?"

"This is last time I come. He say no more," Gabriel began.

Henry interrupted. "Wait. While I have this chance, I want to show you something." He went over to the rough shelf which contained all their manuscripts, picked up his journal, and said slowly, "If we should die here this winter, take all these manuscripts. I trust you to do the right thing with them, especially this one. It's for Adeline." He opened the journal to show some of the drawings he had made in it, and pointed to the dates from the beginning to the previous day.

Gabriel put out his pod. "No, Henry. You not die here. See?" He reached into his satchel, a larger one than he usually carried which bulged to the breaking point, and took out Adeline's letter. "I think. I solve letter problem. Adeline have letter. You have letter."

Henry looked in amazement at the letter. "How did you?"

"Not know words to say how. Listen. Not long talk now. Read letter later." He drew himself listening at Rex's portal. "Colony give credit. He say he not take. Keep you here. Wrong. You not die for Adeline. Live for Adeline. Live for me, even here," he said gesturing around the chamber. "You be free. Take seeds," he continued, removing a sack of seeds from his satchel. "Save for thirteenth time frame. Not know words say why, but save. Sorry I not carry more. Workers give you food, too."

Henry set the seeds down and said, "There is no escape from here."

"You trust me?"

"Yes."

"Work, eat, and live for Adeline. I find answer to problem. Get sliding bead calculator. Ganton waits. We go check charts. I say I need them, get day with you. Soon, he make me train another."

They tapped on the portal. Gabriel held out the sliding bead calculator to show Ganton. They returned to the mine, where Henry and Gabriel spent the day going over the charts and creating more, with Ganton standing behind them, watching everything.

Henry waited until the three of them had been locked in their chamber before saying anything to Herbert and Howard. He didn't want even the tone of his voice to betray Gabriel in the slightest way, because he had sensed from the roach engineer's movements and facial expressions that their situation was very serious.

"We have a true friend in Gabriel," he said, getting the letter from where he had put it in the front of the journal. "I don't know how, but he not only got my letter to Adeline; he managed to get one back to us."

The other two stopped what they were doing and stared. Now that the moment to open it had finally come, Henry's pods shook. He turned to Howard. "Please, open the seal. I'm afraid I'll tear the parchment."

Howard opened the letter and then wrapped himself around Henry to calm him. Henry took the letter and read it.

"My most cherished Henry,

"Do you remember the first day we met? You had been in basic training about two time frames and I had just arrived. Our trainer was called away in some emergency. I remember sitting there, frightened out of my wits, staring at the list of symbols. You put your pod on my thorax, calmed me down and helped me. You tutored me every day until I had caught up to you, and from then on we learned together.

"I didn't know it then, but that was the day I began to cherish you. How could I possibly stop now, and abandon you when you need me the most? My Promised One, I will never abandon you. Nothing can end what I feel for you, not even death.

"None of us here will abandon any of you. Hold on to hope. The colony sent our offer to pay the cost of your return. Regardless of the amount, no one here will allow you to remain there suffering one moment longer than necessary. We were most careful to guard our words, lest our offer betray Gabriel. We must now wait for a reply. Do not despair, any of you. We will have the credit to free you when the traders come at the end of the twelfth time frame.

"Herbert's and Howard's families send their care as well, although they said the letter should be from me to you. All of us here lift up our thoughts that I have followed Gabriel's pictured instructions correctly, and that you will receive this letter. I gain my strength from everyone here and send it to you in my words. I meditate each evening from the eighth to the tenth h-units. May your essence receive my strength in that way, too.

"Forever, faithfully, your Adeline."

20.

*R*outine. It was the only way any of the creatures involved could cope with the eleventh and twelfth time frames, with the exception of Rex, content with the way things were going in Roacheria.

In South Harvester 45, Adeline rose each morning, prodded by her sister, went to the larva nursery, where she poured onto the larvae all the affection she longed to give Henry. When she came home, she ate her supper. At precisely eight h-units, holding Henry's letter in one middle pod, she raised her front pods in contemplation--her sister or her parents took turns joining her. After meditation, Adeline sipped soothing herb tea and went to sleep. On seventhdays, her family met with Herbert's, Howard's, and Henry's families to join all their uplifted thoughts together, then she wandered about the surface at the main entrance to the colony until sundown.

At the Number 6 Mine, Henry, Howard, and Herbert--after being awakened by a warrior banging on the portal--ate a few seeds each morning. Their meager breakfast was barely enough to take the edge off their hunger pangs. Charts in pod, they were escorted by warriors into the producing tunnel, where they directed their crew of five tunnel digging roach workers. Other workers gleaned through the plastic rich dirt, separating plastic from other substances. Still others carted off the sorted materials.

At midday, they stopped for half an h-unit to rest and eat. One of the five diggers would share his lunch. When the work day ended, they were returned to their quarters and locked in. They shared a scanty meal from their fungus patch, which was not growing well, and prepared the next day's tunnel chart.

Their time piece had broken and they could not fix it or get another, so they guessed when it was eight h-units and joined front pods to meditate. Henry always held Adeline's letter to his thorax with one middle pod. After meditating, they fell into an exhausted, hungry sleep.

With his time growing ever shorter, Gabriel rose before dawn, ate as he scurried to the Number 1 Mine where he directed tunnel work all morning and left detailed instructions with the lead digger. He ate a hurried lunch on the way to the Number 6 Mine, directed the placement of timbers in the other two producing tunnels and left careful plans for the lead diggers in those tunnels for the following morning. He spent the evenings working over charts, worrying, and adding images and words to a constantly growing stack of parchment. As the days went on, he worked later and later into the night.

Seventhday afternoons, Gabriel went to the shanties around the Number 6 Mine, where he left as much food and plastic as he could afford to spare with the lead digger in the ants' tunnel. The gifts of plastic for the workers' nymphs insured that they would not betray him. He also explored the area north and west of the mine.

Near the end of the twelfth time frame, he traveled all the way to the border of Roacheria, returning long after dark. He stopped at the Number 6 Mine see how many security warriors Rex kept on duty at night. It was not a large number, but still far more than he could fight off by himself. He had already tried to recruit some of the workers, but they had refused. Their fear of Rex was greater than their sympathy for the plight of the ants. Gabriel understood.

It was nearly midnight and he knew his mate would be worried, but he dragged his pods. Time was growing very short and he still had no idea how he would free his friends. He looked up at the stars and remembered some of the things that Henry had told him about ant life.

There in the meadow, between Number 6 mine and the city of Roacheria, he humbled himself lower than he would for Rex and, with absolute sincerity, spoke to that "source" or "essence" Henry had spoken about so often.

"Whatever exists, with more power than any creature in this world, the ants say you are there. If you understand Roach as well as Ant, please hear me. I am nobody. I am nothing, but I am trying to save them. If there is an answer, let me know it somehow. All my life I have been selfish, but I am trying to be more giving. I do not want to go on if I fail to save their lives. Help me, because I don't know how."

He remained there several minutes listening to the wind rustle the grass around him. Then he rose and slowly returned home.

His mate was waiting for him. "Gabriel, where have you been? I've been worried sick. You haven't been out this late since Last Night Festival. I thought you gave all that up!"

"I'm sorry," he said, caressing her. "I had to do something. I'm not intoxicated, and I won't fall unconscious on the floor like I did then." He remembered how elated he was when this whole mess had begun. He had celebrated until three h-units past midnight and then slept all First Day, which was a day off for every Roacherian worker. The ale . . .   He'd slept . . . And suddenly he had an idea.

*   *   *   *

Commander Ferdinand refused to let Adeline or any of the Council Members go with him to the border bridge at the end of the twelfth time frame. "The safety of every member of this colony is my responsibility," he said. "The plan you approved is too risky to allow anyone but my trained forces. Even the carriers will be sent back after they arrive with the baskets of trade goods. My guards will handle the transfer."

The fire ants arrived early in the morning. Commander Ferdinand ordered nearly two hundred male and female guards fully trained for battle to conceal themselves in the tall meadow grass and bushes. "Keep low and out of sight. At my first whistle, rise and show yourselves. You are to engage in battle only if you hear two whistles. Eat and drink from the supplies in your satchels whenever you feel the need. It may be a long day."

Commander Ferdinand settled himself and ten guards in plain sight of the bridge. They sat in front of the roller carts the roaches had left behind at the end of the tenth time frame when the ants had sent their offer to buy Henry, Herbert, and Howard. The carts were already loaded with seeds, containers of honey and cartons of processed grasshopper to be sent to Roacheria as payment for plastic. The commander placed a metal container next to him filled with ant credit notes the roaches could use for future shipments. "Ransom for our members," he called it.

Near midday, a scout came up to him. "We've spotted them, Commander. It's a very small group, ten traders with the carts, and only twenty warriors. We've searched and searched for movement in the grass, but no one can detect any more. Unless they are behind the carts or among the warriors where we can't see them, Henry, Howard, and Herbert are not with them."

Commander Ferdinand stamped one back pod. "I was really hoping they would be back and our plan wouldn't be necessary. But I'm glad there are so few warriors. I truly want to honor their wish that we not shed life juice for their sake. Pass the word to keep out of sight and be ready."

The traders approached the bridge with the interpreter in the lead. Next to him was a large warrior wearing a crimson ribbon over his head. The ants had never seen such a spectacle before. The roaches did not hesitate, but went on across the bridge and stopped few f-units from where Commander Ferdinand stood.

Commander Ferdinand spoke first. "We are prepared to pay for our members. Here is the credit," he said, gesturing toward the metal box. "Where are they?"

The interpreter said, "The credit will not be necessary. I am afraid I bring you very sad news. This is Ganton, chief of Sir Rudy's son's warriors. As you see, he wears the red ribbon of grief. Your engineers tried to do another controlled collapse to prevent a future disaster for our workers. It went wrong and they were caught up in it. They did not make it out. In view of this loss, Sir Rudy's son pardons their debt."

"Why didn't you notify us sooner?"

"It happened yesterday. They were all set to return with me today but.," the interpreter sighed heavily. Ganton looked at the ground and shook his antennae slowly back and forth, speaking in a somber tone.

"Ganton says that is why so few of us came today," the interpreter said. "Everyone is working to clear the debris. Ganton expresses his sorrow to you. He was responsible for their safety all this time. He says, 'I could protect them from renegades but not from this.' He watched them work every day and knows they were the best at their craft.They did a fine job training Gabriel, who can now work independently. We regret we can't return their bodies."

Rage rose within Commander Ferdinand, but he controlled it. "Their bodies must be returned," he said firmly.

"But," the interpreter stammered, "it might be a long time before we can dig them out, and then the condition . . ."

"I don't care about the condition. You tell your workers to dig. Our engineers could be trapped alive on the inside."

"That is very unlikely. It will take several quarter time frames to uncover them."

"I don't care how long it takes. You will return them. To insure that you do, three of your traders will stay with us."

"In grief, you would take three hostages?" the interpreter asked.

Commander Ferdinand wanted to shout, "*And ours have not been held hostage?*" but he didn't. Instead, he said calmly, "No, not as hostages, as insurance. We don't have much faith in your words any more."

"I'm not authorized to allow that," the interpreter said.

"They can come voluntarily. Our members stayed voluntarily. They will be well treated, and returned the moment our members are back, alive, or in body baskets."

The interpreter spoke back and forth to Ganton, then turned to Commander Ferdinand again. "He says, 'Absolutely not.'"

"I will take them anyway," said Commander Ferdinand. One screeching whistle vibrated from his mandibles.

A brigade of two hundred fire ants rose from their hiding places and stood ready. The roaches froze at the sight of them. They had no desire to commit suicide. Ganton pointed out three of the workers, who were ushered into the charge of several ant guards. The products were transferred and the roaches left the bridge. Warriors took the place of the

workers, straining to pull and push the heavily loaded carts back to Roacheria.

*   *   *   *

Adeline straightened herself on the cushion in Alyssa's work chamber when Commander Ferdinand entered. She knew immediately from the look on his face that her cherished one had not returned and that the news wasn't good.

"Where did you take the roach workers?" Alyssa asked when Commander Ferdinand had finished telling them what had happened.

"They're in the largest prison cubicle. We had prepared it just in case. We put some surface images up on the walls and tried to make it as comfortable as any of our homes. We showed them how to operate the water tap and sanitation facility. They looked frightened, but accepted the food given them."

Adeline said, "Henry is not dead, Commander Ferdinand. They are all alive."

"Adeline, we don't know. We won't know for some time."

"No," she broke in. "They are alive. They have to be, because the thorn bush is still blooming."

"The thorn bush?" Commander Ferdinand turned to Alyssa. "I think she may need another injection of nerve calmers."

"Don't talk about me that way," Adeline said. "I don't need nerve calmers. They are alive, I tell you. Henry's thorn bush is still blooming. When we made our promise, I decided that I would give him the blossom from a thorn bush, because you have to wait so long for the blossom to unfold. But when it does, it's worth the wait, because its fragrance is so sweet and it blooms for a long time. Even when it withers and dies, the fragrance stays. I thought I would have to get a dried one to give him, because we would have our ceremony in winter, when all the thorn bushes are asleep. Then they left and I knew I could get a fresh one, since he would come back in summer."

The others in the chamber stared at Adeline.

"When I came back with you at the end of the sixth time frame, I saw a thorn bush a few hundred f-units off the main entrance trail. It was full of blossoms. I picked one to save for him. After the eighth time frame, the one I picked was withered and dry, but the bush was still blooming. When we came back after the tenth time frame, all the bushes around it had

stopped blooming, but not that one. I looked at it last seventhday and new buds were forming. It's a sign from Essence. Henry is alive, and I will have a fresh blossom to give him."

Commander Ferdinand and Alyssa said nothing. At that moment, neither of them had the heart to tell her that some varieties of thorn bushes continued blooming through the winter, unless it got cold enough for water to freeze on the surface--which didn't happen very often at their latitude. Her first dream about their problems had proven true. Somewhere deep inside, they wanted to believe she was right this time as well.

*   *   *   *

Ganton finished his report and prostrated himself before Rex.

"It's all right, Ganton," Rex said. "I'd have left three, too, with that many fire ants looking at me. Three trade workers are disposable, but we'll keep the ants happy, since they buy so much plastic. Besides, we already talked about what we'd do if they asked for the bodies. How long did the interpreter say it would take us to dig them out?"

"He wasn't specific, Sir, but he implied it would be several quarter time frames."

"Keep them working for another half a time frame. Then leave them locked in their quarters. Don't let anyone give them food or water. We'll send the bodies back right after the new season cycle begins. They ought to be dead by then."

"As you wish, Sir."

*   *   *   *

Around the eighth day of the thirteenth time frame, the lead digger whispered something strange to Henry. It sounded like he was trying to speak Ant: "Gabriel, las neye, sav see."

Henry did not understand what he said, but Gabriel's name was plain, so he knew it was some kind of message meant to give them hope. The lead digger had been giving them lunch every day for quite some time.

*   *   *   *

Gabriel sat quietly trying not to fidget as the physician checked him over. He knew from the workers at the Number 6 Mine that the ants were no longer working, and that Rex would not let anyone into their quarters. The lead digger had been stepped on just for asking. He hoped that they had saved the seeds he had given them the last time he was with Henry, and that he would not find them dead if he was able to carry out his plan.

"What's the problem? You are in perfect physical shape. Why are you wasting my time?" the doctor asked Gabriel.

"I'm having trouble sleeping. I work very long h-units. I come home tired, but I can't get to sleep. A cousin of mine once got a potion to induce sleep for this problem. I would like some of it."

"What work do you do?"

"I'm a mine tunnel engineer."

"Forget, it. You can't afford the potion. Try some ale."

"No, please, I've already tried ale. I do have enough credit. I've been saving. This has been a problem for quite a while now, and I really need some relief," Gabriel begged.

The physician twitched his antennae back and forth. "All right, I'll authorize it. Mix one measure of the powder with water and drink it. You'll be asleep within a quarter h-unit. Don't drink ale when you use this."

"Why not?"

"You'll sleep right through the next day, and when you wake up every part of your body will ache. There will be enough in the packet for ten doses," he said, handing Gabriel the written order to give the clerk.

"Thank you for the warning about the ale," Gabriel said, taking the order and leaving. On the way out of the Medical Center, he gave his last plastic exchange note to the clerk to pay for the visit and the packet of powder.

*   *   *   *

For the first two days that the ants were left alone, they pounded on the portal periodically, and called for an interpreter. They were ignored. The morning of the third day, Henry awoke with a start from a strange dream. He roused the others.

"I figured something out," he began. "I dreamed a lot of memories last night and realized how all the little things Gabriel said and drew fit together. He told us that our colony would buy our freedom, as Adeline said in her letter, and that Sir Rudy's son would not allow it. Do you remember the picture he drew of himself listening at that portal? Then he gave me those seeds and said to save them for the thirteenth time frame, but he didn't have the words to say why. That's what that worker was trying to tell me the other day: 'Last Night. Save seeds.' I think Sir Rudy's son plans to let us starve to death."

Howard stared at him. "Wouldn't it be easier to return us for the credit?"

"He won't want our colony to know how we have been treated. Think about it! He can't let us live."

Herbert slumped down and groaned.

"Howard, we did save those seeds, didn't we?" Henry asked.

"Yes," Howard answered.

"Gabriel has always said he'd find a way. I'm sure that digger was trying to say 'Last Night.' Maybe that's when Gabriel plans to free us. Will our supplies hold out that long?"

"I don't know," replied Howard.

They gathered everything they had, measuring their water supply carefully. When they looked at the meager amount, Howard said, "In the northern colonies, when the winter is the coldest and the surface is covered with frozen sky water, colony members go to the deepest areas to special chambers and enter winter inactivity. They group together for warmth, eat little and sleep most of the time. That's how they have survived for ages. We need to do something like that now. It isn't that cold, but we should put our sleep cushions together, huddle with each other and cover ourselves with all our coverlets. Each time we wake up, we will eat and drink only enough to be able to sleep again. If Gabriel isn't able to free us, the day will come when we won't wake up, but it won't be painful."

On the day that they consumed the last of their food and water, they remained awake a little longer. Henry made an entry in his journal and hoped that Gabriel would be the one to find it.

> "I don't know what day this is. Our food and water are gone. We have done everything we can. Please, forgive me, Adeline. I have always cherished you. I never thought things would turn out this way."

They meditated together, chanting the Last Day songs and reciting their creed, even though they weren't sure if it was Last Day. Then they curled up and went to sleep.

21.

*A*deline and her father walked home from Last Day meditation together. The rest of the family had gone on ahead. Adeline had stayed to meditate alone. She had managed not to let one tear fall during the service, focusing all her thoughts on Henry.

"Adeline, please," her father said, "we are all concerned about you. Let yourself grieve. Think about the others. Herbert's family and Howard's daughter were very hurt when you refused to attend the memorials for them last sixthday. Henry's parents want to set a date for his."

Adeline turned to her father, mandibles set. "I told them then and I'll repeat it now. I won't participate in a service for the dead when they are still alive. The vision in my first dream was right, and so is this one. Henry's thorn bush still has life." She would not admit, even to herself, that the bush was nearly dormant. One last stem with one bud and three leaves were all that remained. To that last bit, Adeline clung in hope.

Her father shook his head and said nothing more.

       *   *   *   *

"Come in, Ganton," Rex said, holding open the portal to his work chamber. "Are both mines secure?"

"Yes, Sir. I only left five on guard at each mine, though. That's the number we had last season cycle for Last Night festival and there were no problems. Those chosen complained about not being able to celebrate."

"Tell them they can have two days off instead of just First Day, and I'll give them the ale for their late celebration. That ought to help. What are your plans?"

"I'll be at the Public House with friends."

"The Supreme Executor's head of security?"

"Yes, Sir, how did you know?"

"He mentioned it when he invited me to the Board Member party at his home. Here," he handed Ganton several credit exchange notes. "A reward for your loyalty. Have a good celebration, but check in with me in the evening on First Day."

"Thank you, Sir," Ganton said, glancing at the denominations of the exchange notes. He'd be able to sponsor many rounds of ale with that amount. "Have a great time now that you've declared your mourning over."

*   *   *   *

Gabriel put his front pods on his head. "I don't feel well," he said to his mate. "Why don't you go on to the party at the mine overseer's house without me. I'll take care of our nymphs."

His mate looked at him. "Are you sure? We've both been looking forward to this. He's never invited us before."

"Yes, I'm sure. But you go have a good time." Gabriel gave her a gentle push. She went out their portal and down the path, then stopped and looked back.

Gabriel bent and rubbed his head. "Go on. I'll be fine. I just need some sleep." He watched her go and then closed the portal.

Both nymphs were asleep in their safety cages. He checked the latches. They couldn't get out by accident. They'd never know he was gone.

He placed a thick stack of parchments into the bottom of his satchel while he waited for the water to boil. Then he added the herbs to the pot and let it sit. Carefully, he dumped the powder the doctor had given him into a jug of ale and replaced the stopper. He swished it a little so the powder would mix and dissolve, and added two metal mugs to his satchel. He poured the tea into an insulated container and put it and a sack of seeds in his satchel with everything else. He was about ready to leave when his mate returned.

"I didn't want you to be alone," she said. "So I came home." She looked at the jug he held in one pod and his satchel slung over his back. "Gabriel, what are you doing? Where were you going to go? You said you were sick."

Gabriel's antennae drooped. "I'm not going to a festival. I have something I have to do."

"What? I'm tired of all this nonsense. You're keeping another female, I know it. Credit keeps disappearing around here and you're always late. I want the truth," she cried.

"Believe me, I don't have another female. It's safer for both of us if you don't know."

"Safer! What are you doing, Gabriel?"

Gabriel set the jug down. "Do you trust me?"

"No, not at this particular moment."

"Have you come to care about me more this season cycle? I know I have learned to care very deeply for you."

She sighed. "Yes, I have. Would I be this upset with you and come home from a festival, if I didn't?"

"Sit down," he said, and then he told her what he intended to do.

She stared at him, speechless.

"Please, try to understand. I can't let them die after all they've done here. It's wrong, plain wrong. If I can do something and I don't, then I'm just as bad as Sir Rex. Can't you see that?"

"But what happens to me and your daughters if you get caught?"

"Rex won't condemn me because he needs me to build his cursed tunnels and train others. He'll hurt me, but he won't kill me. My death would cost him too much credit. Don't forget the Certificate of Assurance I got from him. Do you remember where it is?"

"Yes," her voice shook. "Gabriel, please, don't do this."

"I must. Listen, if The Enforcers do come, don't try to cover for me. Since you insisted on knowing the truth, tell them I set the ants free. Remember what I told you about the Formal Inquiry and what Rachel said? You must do that to, if you need to." He put his pods around her and stroked her. "It's getting late. I have to leave."

Gabriel hurried along small back lanes away from his domicile and into nearby fields. It was a longer route to the Number 6 Mine that way, but he wanted to avoid other roaches who might recognize him or ask why he was carrying a satchel. The jug of ale was not a problem on this night, but the satchel would definitely arouse curiosity.

He looked up at the sky, regretting that he had no time to humble himself and to speak to it, as he had frequently during the thirteenth time frame. He never heard it speak back, but he always felt stronger and more confident afterward, and that was something he couldn't explain. As he ran along he whispered to the wind, "Sorry I don't have time to be more formal. Thank you that this night is clear, so the stars will guide their journey. Please, let them be alive."

He approached the mine from the south. The night he had counted, there had been ten warriors on duty: four pairs of two around the mine pit and two at the portal of the ants' quarters. He took the stopper off the jug of ale and poured a little of it over his outer mandibles and down his front, then sauntered up to the first guard post, singing a Last Night song badly.

"Raise you mug and be of good cheer,
The end of the season cycle's finally here . . ."

Swinging the jug toward the warrior, surprised and relieved that there was only one, he said slowly, "Stuck out here with no celebration, hmmm? Well, I brought it to you. Have a mug with me?"

"I'm on duty."

"So? What could happen tonight? Who else is here? We'll all celebrate."

The warrior hesitated. "He'll find out."

"How?" Gabriel persisted. "Do you think either Ganton or Sir Rex will come out here and check on you? Not a chance. How will they know? I'm not going to tell them. Are you?"

The warrior smiled. "No, of course not. What have you got there?"

"The best ale available. Very different flavor. Watch out, it has a real kick to it," he said, filling the mugs.

As the warrior drank the ale, Gabriel staggered backwards, spilling it on himself. "Oops," he laughed, and sat down.

The warrior finished his off and sat down, holding the mug out for more. "You're right, this is very good."

Gabriel filled it again and they laughed their way through the rest of the song Gabriel had been singing whan he approached:

"Now we can forget the past,

Nothing here will ever last.

Look ahead, it's got to be better . . ."

The warrior slumped over, the sounds of heavy sleep rasping away from his mandibles in place of the song. Gabriel shook him, realizing that the powder had worked very quickly with the ale. There was no response. Luck, or some other force was with him. It would take only half the time he had planned to subdue the guards, which made up for his late start. He picked up the jug and the mugs and headed for the post on the western side of the pit.

The same tactic worked for both the western and northern rim posts. By the time he approached the eastern post, which was within sight of the ants' quarters, his exoskeleton reeked of ale. He had carefully thought out a way to get the rim warrior and the portal guard to come together, but as he drew closer, he saw it wasn't necessary. The two warriors were already together, half way between their posts, complaining to each other about being stuck on duty.

They proved to be the easiest, and within a few minutes, both were sound asleep. Gabriel stopped briefly at the water pump to rinse the sticky ale off himself and hurried over to the portal. He slid the locking bar out of its notches quietly, his whole body quaking, his breathing heavy. An odor greeted him as he opened the portal. He sighed with relief. It was not the smell of death.

Lowering his antennae to guide him through the dark, he entered the chamber, calling their names. There was no reply, but he could sense their nearness and made his way toward a large mass in the center of the chamber. He realized that it was their sleep cushions, pushed together. He lifted the coverlets and reached out. His pod touched Henry first. Gently, he shook Henry's thorax with one pod while he drew the tea from his satchel with another.

Visions of Adeline passed in and out of Henry's mind, calling to him. He felt a touch, but wanted it to go away, reaching out to his vision and whispering, "Adeline, Adeline."

The touch turned to a shake and a voice disturbed his dream. "No, I, Gabriel. Henry, please, come."

Still not fully awake, Henry felt himself lifted. A mug came near his mouth, filling him with its warm aroma.

"Drink," he heard.

It took several sips for him to fully realize what was happening. "Gabriel," he said. "You really came."

"I find answer," Gabriel whispered. "Take mug now."

Henry rolled over and took the mug in his front pods, while Gabriel roused Herbert and Howard. Gabriel indicated that they should not turn on a lantern. There in the dark, Gabriel handed them seed after seed. For the first time in many time frames, they ate until they were satisfied.

Gabriel gestured toward all their belongings, picked up only their water flasks, and said, "Leave here. Come now."

They started out the portal, but Henry turned back. "Wait!" he said. "My journal."

He fumbled through the manuscripts on the shelf until he found it and joined them. Gabriel reached out for it and managed to fit it into his satchel.

They followed Gabriel to the water pump, filled the flasks and headed into the night. Henry glanced toward the warriors, flat on their backs on the ground. "Gabriel, are they dead?" he asked.

"No," Gabriel whispered back. "Sleep long time."

Gabriel led them away from the mine, avoiding its shanties and then changed course. They followed in silence without question, at as rapid a pace as they could manage in their weakened condition. After an h-unit, Gabriel stopped to rest. He handed them the flask of tea again and passed out some more seeds.

"Safe here," he said.

A short time later, they resumed their journey. Henry saw Gabriel gazing at the stars as they went along and wondered why. Gabriel stopped them at the edge of a pond.

"Go this way," he said, leading them the long way around it. "Spider there," he said, pointing the other way.

Much later, he stopped them again to rest. As they drank from the flasks, he talked to Henry. "Number 1 Mine back that way," he pointed. "We go about fifteen d-units to now. You go this way. See small water once, then deep sides and water." He gestured to indicate the shape of the stream. "That end of Roacheria. You cross, then follow water. Take you home."

He moved behind Henry. "Look sky." He reached into the air with his front pod, traced the shape of a star group, and pointed to an especially bright one. "See?"

Henry nodded.

"You here," Gabriel said, facing the direction they should go. He pointed to the bright star again and said, "Keep it here," pointing to his right side. "Understand?"

Henry nodded, and said, "Gabriel, I don't know how to thank you. What will he do to you?"

Gabriel shook his antennae. "Not problem. You teach me. He needs me. You go home. Cherish Adeline. I think of you and smile."

Henry took his front pods in friendship, wishing that somehow they would see each other again someday, and knowing it would never be possible. "I will not forget you," he said.

"I remember you and problems you teach me. I learn much more than tunnels. Ants learn now," he handed Henry his satchel. "More food here and gift. You learn our words. Never this again."

"What?"

"You see later. Take and go. Night goes fast," he said pointing them on their way, but he hesitated. "Henry, Howard, Herbert, please, I'm sorry. All this wrong to you, so wrong."

"It was never your fault, but if you feel the need to be forgiven, then I forgive you. You risked yourself to make things right again," Henry said, embracing him and taking the satchel from him.

Howard and Herbert embraced Gabriel, and then he left them, turning back the way they had come.

Herbert looked at Henry. "I hope you understood which way to go. I've never traveled alone on the surface, and never at night."

"We're to keep heading this way," Henry said, taking the lead, "keeping that bright star on our right. We will cross one small stream, and then later, reach the border stream. All we have to do from there is follow it the way the water flows."

"How many d-units do you think it is?" Howard asked.

"I'm not sure."

After traveling perhaps a quarter h-unit, they saw a dim light ahead of them and heard the familiar sounds of the Roach language. They dropped into the meadow grass in silence.

When the sounds came no closer, Henry whispered, "I'm going to crawl up that wood plant and take a look."

He made his way to a wood plant several f-units from them, and started up it's thick center stem. It should have been an easy climb, but Henry's pods kept slipping. His muscles were weak from malnutrition and the inactivity the last half time frame. When he finally struggled to the top, he looked toward the source of the light and the voices.

Ahead, 200 f-units he guessed, a group of six male and two female roaches lay around a fire, laughing and drinking from three jugs of ale. Two of them ate sloppily from a sack. He watched a moment or two more, to rest and to be sure they were unaware of things outside the circle of fire light, and then, clinging to the center of the wood plant, made his way down and back to his friends.

"There are six males," he whispered, "warrior sized, probably renegades. They seem to be intoxicated and aren't paying attention to anything but two females. I watched one of the males stroke a female in a most inappropriate way. Even if they are mated, to act that way in front of others..."

"Mark my words," Howard whispered, "if the roaches don't learn to care for one another with respect, they will surely go the way of the Duo Pods."

"If we make a wide circle, we'll pass them with ease," Henry continued.

Henry led them in a wide arc around the light, then checked their direction with the star, so they could continue their journey westward. Not long after that, they came to the small stream Gabriel had described. It proved to be very shallow and easy to cross, barely getting them wet past their first appendage joints. They reached the border stream in good spirits, all things considered.

"I can see why it makes such a good border," Henry remarked. "The banks are steeper and deeper here than they are at the bridge. We should be very cautious. I didn't say this before, but I had trouble climbing the wood plant. My middle and back pods felt very weak, and I could barely get a grip on the rough bark. This slope has nothing to grip. Maybe we should go along this side and look for a better place."

Howard shook his head. "I've never traveled it, but many have said that it gets no better. The bridge is the best there is, but if we go that far on this side, we may be seen and who knows what might happen. The water is only six f-units across, and not all that deep, so I've been told. I'll take my chances here."

"Let's at least go down backwards. See where those branches are piled up across the water? We could grab them to guide ourselves across," Henry said, situating the satchel more securely on the back of his thorax.

Henry turned himself abdomen first and began his descent. Herbert followed. Howard, saying that he felt strong enough, began head first, slipped immediately and went tumbling head over abdomen down the slope, landing in the pile of brush with a groan.

"Howard, are you all right?" Henry asked, reaching him a moment later.

"Ugh," Howard groaned. "Weakness blurred my mind. I should have listened to you. I think I broke my leg again. The pain is like fire."

Herbert looked on helplessly. "What can we do? We've no binding material or anything!"

Howard looked up at them, gritting his mandibles together, and rasped, "There's no way you could get me up that slope. Leave me here. Save yourselves."

Henry was firm. "No, I won't leave you here, not after all we've been through. We'll manage somehow. Herbert, see if you can find a good straight branch in this tangle of brush. I'll pull some grass and braid it into a band to tie the splint. But first, let me make sure you have no other injuries, Howard."

He found that Howard's appendage was badly broken, much worse than the first time, and his main support joint was twisted, which was why the pain was so bad. He moved Howard only enough to free him from the brush and make room to work. The flat space from the bottom of the bank to the water's edge was extremely narrow. If the weather hadn't been so dry lately, there would have been no ledge at all.

Henry grabbed at several long grass stems and began braiding them together. Herbert reached in and out of the brush pile until he found a straight branch with the right thickness and then began helping Henry.

"It's not the best binding, but it will have to do," Henry said. "Herbert, you go across the stream first. I'll lift Howard and hand him to you. Then I'll follow. Howard, grip this stick in your mandibles. It won't stop the pain when we move you, but it's better than nothing."

"Henry, the water is frigid," Herbert said as he started across. "I can't find the bottom. Hold onto the branches." In a moment, he was on the other bank.

Henry moved Howard gently into the water, holding him with his front pods and gripping a branch with one middle pod. He pushed Howard ahead of himself. "Hold out your front pod, so Herbert can reach you," he said.

Herbert reached as far as he could without falling in and managed to grab Howard's extended pod, and pulled him to the bank. Henry finished his crossing with relative ease. After resting a moment, Henry looked up the steep bank.

"Wait here while I see how slippery it is," he said, pulling himself up a bit. "May The Essence be praised. The dried mud on this side is not quite so slippery. We can dig our pods in and climb up. Herbert, you hold Howard's abdomen. I'll support his head and thorax. I know we can do this."

At the pace of a crawling shelled creature, they made their way up the steep bank, bearing Howard's weight with their front pods, digging their middle and back ones into the bank, pod over pod, until they reached the top. With one last effort, they lifted Howard over the edge and set him down on the meadow grass on The Colonies' side of the stream. Exhausted, they flopped down beside him. Howard had bit through the stick.

Henry knew from the look in Herbert's eyes how spent he was, but neither of them said a word. Henry pulled himself up and looked around. Meadows spread out on all sides. In the distance, tall, dark shapes loomed into the night sky--groves of wood plants. Nothing moved in the meadow grass, but he remembered that Deanna's mate had been on night watch when he and his partner were killed by a mantis. He lifted up silent thoughts for their safety and asked for enough strength to make it home.

"I'm going to see what Gabriel has given us," he said at last.

He opened the satchel and took out the flask of tea. There was a little bit left, which he offered to Howard. Next, he removed a small sack of seeds, twice as much as they had had in a day for the last several time frames.

"The rest is all parchment," he said, taking out the top piece. He strained to look at it in the scant light of the moon and stars, then drew out another and another. "So this is what he meant, 'You learn our words', he's made us a picture dictionary of the Roach language!"

Herbert roused himself. "What?"

"Look," Henry handed him the top sheet. "He's printed the word in Roach and drawn a picture to show its meaning. There's a huge stack here. He must have been working on this for a long time."

Henry put the parchments carefully back in the satchel. "We've got enough food. I've no idea how much farther it is, but we've used enough time. We should go as far as we can before it gets light."

"You'll make better time without me," Howard said. "I'll be all right here. Leave a few seeds and a flask of water. You can send someone back for me when you reach home."

Henry looked at Herbert, who shook his head. "No," Henry replied, "We'll carry you. This is level ground, so it will be easier. We won't leave you out here by yourself for some predator to find."

"I'll take you first," Herbert said, lifting Howard gently. "It will be easier if we take turns."

As their trek continued, their pace became slower, their turns shorter, and their rests more frequent. Henry's appendage muscles began to swell with strain, but he had lost so much body mass that they didn't press painfully outward against his exoskeleton. Herbert's eyes showed pain and determination. On they struggled.

"It can't be much farther," Henry said as the sky began to lighten.

"Look!" shouted Herbert, when the light allowed them to see into the distance. "Grasshoppers, a whole herd of them, there, off to our right! We must be near one of the dairies. We're saved!"

The mere sight of something familiar gave them a brief surge of energy. They staggered toward the herd, shouting as loudly as they could. Moments later they found themselves surrounded by several dairiers and fire ant guards.

"They told us you were dead," Henry heard someone say before he collapsed from exhaustion.

*   *   *   *

Adeline moved slowly from one larva coop to the next. She hummed softly as she stroked each of the larvae in her care. They had finished their late-morning feeding of finely ground plastic mixed with honey dew. Each of her five charges had lapped it from her pods greedily. Now, one by one, they dropped off to sleep as she stroked them. A lump welled up inside her, but she pushed it back. She would not let herself lose control again. There had been moments lately when she doubted her sanity.

After she stroked the last larva to sleep, she felt a pod on her thorax. The nursery supervisor had been stroking her more and more lately. Adeline pulled away a little, worried that her supervisor might think she was incompetent. Maybe she was.

The touch was more firm. "Adeline," she heard and turned around to see Alyssa there, smiling. "Adeline, come with me. You were right. They are alive! Gabriel helped them escape. He guided them for several d-units and pointed their way to the border stream. They followed it until they came to Outlying Dairy Mound 10 at the end of the northeast tunnel. Guards found them among the grasshoppers at dawn. Three dairiers brought them here half an h-unit ago took them directly to the Medical Center."

Adeline could find no words. Her supervisor appeared at the portal and said, "I'll take over. Go on, Adeline," and embraced her in joy.

The two females raced through the tunnels to the Medical Center. Upon reaching it, Adeline said, "Where is he? Please, take me to my Henry."

A medical attendant smiled and said, "This way, but the doctor would like to talk to you first."

Adeline followed the attendant into a small chamber where she was told to make herself comfortable. Her heart pounded. She could not be comfortable. The doctor entered, smiling.

"Henry will be fine in time," she began. "He's suffering from extreme exhaustion and mild carrier strain syndrome, brought on by near starvation. All of them have lost about one fourth of their body mass. Another day or two and they would have died. It's amazing that they made it back. Howard has a badly broken appendage and is in surgery. Herbert and Henry are asleep. I'll take you to Henry. You may stay with him as long as you like. I must keep him here for several days, until he begins to gain weight on a supplemental nourishment program. Full recovery will take a few time frames."

She took Adeline's front pod in hers and led her into a small clinic chamber. Adeline walked over to the thistledown mattress where Henry lay, and wrapped herself around him.

He stirred and opened his eyes. "Am I dreaming again, or am I home?" he asked.

"You're home," she said, and began to cry.

22.

*I*n the evening on First Day, Ganton went to see Sir Rex.

"Sir, we have a problem. I went out to the mine to give the guards relief and the ale I promised them. I decided to check and see if it was time to start the funeral procession. The portal guard and the east rim guard were sound asleep. I had difficulty waking them. When I finally did, they screamed in pain. The ants' chamber was empty! The portal guard said Gabriel was out there and gave them funny tasting water. He couldn't remember anything else."

"Bring that piece of fly bait, Gabriel, to me at once. Then tear those two guards apart in front of the others as an example. Let them know more pain than they ever thought possible."

          *   *   *   *

Gabriel had gotten home around two h-units after midnight. His mate cried with relief when he came in the portal. They talked about the different things that might happen and what she should do in each scenario before going to sleep. Gabriel slept more peacefully than he had in several time frames.

When Ganton barged in without knocking, Gabriel stood and faced him calmly. "I know why you are here. You don't have to drag me. I'll come with you." Then he turned to his mate. "It's all right. It's only Ganton. Remember what I said."

When they reached Sir Rex's work chamber at the Number 1 Mine, Gabriel did not prostrate himself. It wouldn't have done any good. Instead, he looked directly into Sir Rex's eyes, feeling better about himself than he ever had in his life. Then he lay down on his back and waited for the torture he knew would come.

Rex's rage lasted a long time. Gabriel did not cry out, not even once. When Rex finally stopped, and every joint and vulnerable area Gabriel had throbbed with pain, he realized the secret of the ants' strength. When you lived your life for someone else, you could bear anything.

"Get up," Rex demanded. "You will say nothing of this to anyone, and you had better hope that South Harvester Colony 45 does not send fire ants in revenge. Because, if they do, you'll be out in front. You will begin training my cousin and the other trainee tomorrow and act as if nothing happened. Ganton will be watching you closely. Now get out of my sight!"

Gabriel staggered out and went home.

The following day, the three traders who had been kept in South Harvester 45 arrived with a message. Rex sent for an interpreter.

"To the Son of Sir Rudy,

"Our members have arrived home. Although it is obvious that they have been severely mistreated, it is their wish that we not pursue justice for them. We hereby return those who stayed with us voluntarily until this matter was settled. South Harvester 45 Council."

Rex sent a message to the Supreme Executor of the S.E.R.C.B. "The problem with South Harvester 45 is settled. Never mention it again in any Board meeting or in future formal communications with The Combined Colonies."

*   *   *   *

On the last day of the first time frame, exactly one season cycle from the date they had originally planned, Henry and Adeline stood before their family and friends to begin their mating ceremony. Henry had regained some of his body mass. He was still weak, but was able to work part of each day.

He stood proudly before his Promised One and handed her his symbolic gift, a pod-sized rock, with her letter wrapped around it. "You are the rock of my strength. You stood by me solidly and never cracked or broke. I come to you now, to give you myself and begin to fulfill our promise, because I will cherish you with the strength of this rock."

Facing him, she reached out and handed him a freshly cut blossom from the thorn bush, with his letter wrapped around the stem. "Life is full of the pain of thorns. But once you get beyond them, and wait patiently for the blossom to open, it's more than worth it, because its exquisite fragrance lasts forever. I come to you now, to give you myself and begin to fulfill our promise because you are worth waiting for."

The rest of their ceremony proceeded exactly as Henry had described it to Gabriel so many time frames before.

Four time frames later, fully recovered, Henry held their first hatched daughter close to his thorax. The tiny larva wiggled and squeaked as Henry waited for Adeline to tell their families and friends what name she would give their daughter.

Ant mothers usually followed one of two traditions when naming their larvae. One way was to honor the memory of a family member who had died. Another was that the first hatched would be given the mother's name, or the male version of it.

Adeline smiled. "I'm going to do things a little differently. Our daughter will be called Henrietta, for her father. May she grow to have all his emotional strength and endurance, his charity and compassion, his humility and mercy, and everything else that makes him great among us."

Pods drummed the floor in approval. When it grew quiet, Henry said, "May she live all her life within the safety of this colony's tunnels. May she never know the pain of betrayal, or the treachery and greed of Roacheria."

*   *   *   *

Howard lived a quiet retirement with his daughter and her mate, helping care for their young. He died of natural causes five season cycles later.

Henry's friendship with Herbert grew stronger. The following season cycle, Herbert mated. Many season cycles later, his first son mated

Henry's second daughter, bringing the families even closer. Henry became South Harvester Colony 45's chief tunnel engineer, and was a mentor to many.

The picture dictionary of the Roach language, written by Gabriel, became the basis for a few in each colony learning to read Roach. All the colonies requested everything be written down very precisely in every agreement with Roacheria, and it became much more difficult for Roacheria to deceive any colony, at least on parchment.

Ten season cycles later, The Colonies invented a system for transmitting words and images to distant receiving screens, called video walls, using lightning bug power, and another device that preserved spoken words, called a voice imager. In the interests of better communication, they shared the devices with Roacheria, so that future problems between the Combined Colonies of Insectia and Organized Roacheria could be resolved expediently and peacefully.

Rufus' mate never laid any other eggs. She lived her life quietly, raising their son on the credit he had saved. Their son did become an interpreter, and worked for The Board when it made an agreement for a joint archaeological project with the ants many season cycles later. His name was Randal.

Gabriel trained several other roaches over the next four season cycles in what later became known throughout Roacheria as the science of "Antunology." As it spread throughout the region, accidental deaths in the mines dropped seventy-five percent.

Sir Rex rented Gabriel to Sir Ronald, who owned the Number 2 Mine. One day, when Sir Ronald came to settle a dispute between the workers, a fight broke out. Sir Ronald was badly injured and Gabriel was killed. A Formal Inquiry ruled that Sir Ronald should be the one to pay Gabriel's mate's Certificate of Assurance, but denied Sir Rex further compensation for the loss of an employee. They never sorted out who instigated the fight, but Sir Ronald insisted that Rex had had a part in it.

Sir Rex never achieved his ambition of becoming the Supreme Executor of the S.E.R.C.B., but he dictated policy through continued treachery and with the number of votes he controlled, ruling in fact rather than name. Many season cycles later, Rex grew weary of waiting for Sir Rodger to end his opposition to Rex's policies. He used Rachel to plant evidence against Sir Rodger and managed to get him banished. He laughed when Sir Rodger's parting words echoed what he had said long ago in Rex's work chamber, "Sooner or later, in one way or another, everything we do comes back to us." Sir Rodger's vote was given to his son-in-law, Sir Reginald, not to Sir Rex. Sir Rodger wandered off into the surface area around the dead South Dairy Colony 50.

Afterword:
Henry Roach-Dairier

It took me over a season cycle to research and write the manuscript of *To Build A Tunnel*. It would have gone faster, had I not been so busy with my training groups. There was one puzzle I couldn't figure out: the script on the outside of the package containing Gabriel's journal did not match his script inside.

Throughout all of it, Ruth, who had given me Gabriel's journal, continued in my training group. I kept myself open, wondering what her connection to Gabriel was, and hoping she would tell me more about herself. I asked her to remain after the others left on several occasions, thanked her for giving me the journal, and kept her posted on my research and writing, but she never said anything.

I respected her privacy, but I had to know. The training facility records stated her domicile location and parents' names. Using that, I checked all the hatching and death records at the Agency for Document Registration. I learned that her parents' names were Richard and Ginger, and that their domicile had originally belonged to Gabriel. Richard was the son of Gallo, who was the son of Griffin, Gabriel's brother.

When I finished the manuscript, I felt a need to know more, and decided to call on them. I made a special copy of my work for them and tapped gently on their portal one seventhday afternoon.

Ruth answered the portal. "Trainer Henry, what brings you here? It's good to see you."

"Thank you, Ruth. Are your parents in?"

She gestured for me to enter and introduced me to her parents and her grandfather, Gallo, who lived with them.

"Good afternoon," I said, stooping low in resect. "Please, pardon my intrusion into the privacy of your home. I thought you might appreciate a copy of my work before I present it for publication. If I've gotten too personal, I'll revise it."

Richard took the stack of parchment from me and swept his pod over the surface. Then he handed it to Gallo.

I continued. "I want to thank you for leading me to search for the whole truth. I felt the need to be here in this dwelling. Gabriel was a real hero, and I would not exist, if he hadn't acted so selflessly long ago."

"Come closer, please, young male," Gallow said, "I don't see very well any more."

I drew close to him and he felt my features. "You're a roach!" he exclaimed.

"Didn't Ruth tell you?" I asked.

"No, she never says much," he replied, glaring at her.

I explained my family background.

"Times change," he said, when I finished. "It has been many season cycles since I've thought of these things. My uncle paid a high price for that selfless act."

"I know," I said. "It's time he was properly honored."

Ruth arranged her grandfather's cushions so he would be more comfortable and brought him a mug of ale. "My father, Griffin, was Gabriel's brother. He found the journal after Gabriel was killed. He is the one who wrapped it up and wrote that inscription on the outside. He hid it and told Gabriel's mate she should never speak of it if she valued her life. She took the amount of the Certificate of Assurance in one sum and left this area. No one ever found out where she went. When my father was old and dying, he said to me, 'I think he's dead, now. You can get out the journal.' The problem was that he never told anyone where he'd hidden it. I guess the ones you really need to thank are my mischievous grandsons."

We laughed and talked of simple things. I told them a little more about my past, and about my dreams for the future. I promised to return and tell them more about my grandfather, Antony. I left with a great feeling of peace.

The Chronicles of Henry Roach-Dairier Continue:

New South Dairy Colony 50, the second book of the trilogy, opens with Henry as a nymph, in a coma after accidentally ingesting a bad combination of medicines in his physician father's lab. His ant grandfather, Antony Dairier, decides it's time to straighten out his grandson. He reveals to Henry the details of his own life: the war and the emotional pain which resulted in his dedication to the ideal of the experimental ant/roach colony, New South Dairy 50.
ISBN 0-9753410-2-2

The Re-creation of Roacheria, the final book of the trilogy, tell's Henry's own story. The adult Henry is an enigma. Most members of New South Dairy 50 consider him too roach-like, even after he grows beyond the high junx of his youth. Influential roaches consider his ways of Antism, and the fact that he is of mixed variety, dangerous to their power sturcture. Hatreds dating back to the days of his great-grandfather rise again in an attempt to destroy him and the community that is dedicated to the ways of his ant grandfather, Antony, and which Henry seeks to build in Roacheria. Henry and his supporters realize that if the two species cannot come together in true peace, they will bring themselves to the same end as the Duo Pods—extinction.
ISBN 0-9753410-3-0

APPENDIX

Time Line of Major Events

SEASON CYCLE

Roach (O.R.)   Combined Colonies f Insectia (C.C.I.)

Roach (O.R.)		Combined Colonies f Insectia (C.C.I.)
1		Enslavement of border colonies by Roacheria
33	1	Beginning of the Combined Colonies, violent conflict to free enslaved colonies
177	144	Rex Hatches in Roacheria
198	165	Death of South Dairy 50; Antony Dairier hatches
201	168	Rex enslaves Henry, Howard and Herbert
212	179	Antony emerges from pupation as an adult
213	180	Sir Rodger banished from Roacheria
219	186	Beginning of Ant/Roach Archeological project, Henrietta's mentorship, Murder of Antony's family, Violent conflict with Roacheria
221	188	Peace with Roacheria, Henrietta and Antony mate
222	189	Establishment of New South Dairy 50
245	212	Death of Rex
257	224	Death or Henrietta, hatching of Henry Roach-Dairier
275	242	Death of Anthony
279	246	Henry establishes Meadow Commonwealth

Genealogy Charts

The Ant Families

Gen.1 Howard

Gen. 2   David/Dorothy   **Henry/Adeline**   Herbert/Corina   Cort

Gen.3 Arthur, **Antony**,   **Henrietta,** Hilda, Annie   Corin   Art/Allie
    Drew, Arlene, Allen,   Andrew

Gen 4. **Rodger** /Genny Roach (sister of Rayanne)   Corina/Al
    (adopted by Antony and Henrietta)

Gen.5 David, Dorothy, Arthur, Drew,
        Henry/Regina   Adeline-**Dell**/Donald

Gen. 6   Gabrielle and sibblings

The Roach Families

Gen. 1 **Sir Rudy**/mate (brothers) Sir Royal/mate
              (numerous descendents not specifically mentioned)

Gen.2 **SirRex**, Rolinda   **Gabriel**/mate (brothers)   Griffin/mate
        Regina/mate
Gen. 3   Rudy/mate   Gabrielle-Genette, Rochelle-Riley   Gallo

Gen.4.   **Robert**/   Rebecca   Richard/Ginger
       (not aware of her relationship to Rochelle)
Gen. 5 **Regina**-mate of **Henry Roach-Dairier**   Ruth (mate of **Rundell)**
                            Gallo, Griffen

Gen. 6   Gabrielle

Gen. 1 **Sir Rodger**

Gen.   4 daughters of Sir Rodger, youngest mates Sir reginald
        Sir Reginald   **MaterRoland/Ralyn**   **Sir Ronald**/mate

Gen. 3 Sir Reginald   three sons,   daughter, **Geree'/George**
       (the Younger) late life son, **Rick/Genelle**   **Rodger/Ginny**
Gen. 4 various descendants
      not specifically mentioned

Gen. 5   Ray/Ramona   **Henry Roach-Dairier**

                                     And sibblings

Other Characters
not necessarily related to each other
included so the reader may relate to approximate age of contemporaries

Gen. 1 **Master Gerard**/mate   **Sir Rolo/Rachael**

Gen. 2.   **Master/Sir Raphael**   son   **Master Diandra**

Gen. 3 **Renee**/ Rita   **Gerry**/ Rayanne (Gen.4 Ginny's sister)

Gen. 4 3 nymphs **Sir Reese**   son Master Riedel Trainer Renard

Gen 5.   **Reese** (book 3)   **Gatlin**   **Rusty**